The Author Tony Robins

To Brenda · x x
2/7/13

Printed by Flaydemouse.
Yeovil. Somerset

Acknowledgments.

To my lovely wife Audrey for putting up with me spending hours on the computer. I would like to dedicate these stories to my grandfather's brother. Great Uncle Lionel Nethaniel (Tinker or Nat) Robins

The characters in these stories are entirely imaginary and bear no resemblance to any person living or dead and I have only used local Dorset names for the benefit of the story.

Golden Cap the highest sea cliff on the South coast at 626 feet

THE UNKNOWN DORSET AT WAR.

Humorous stories of the Second World War in South Dorset.

And other War Time Stories.

By Tony Robins

' *If the British Empire and its commonwealth last for a*
thousand years, men will still say.'
" *This was their finest hour.* "   *Winston Churchill. P.M. 1940.*

War was declared on Sunday the 3rd of September 1939, when Neville Chamberlain the British Prime Minister made an announcement on the radio to the British people on Sunday morning at quarter past eleven.
'The British Government has informed the German Ambassador in London, that the German forces must leave Poland immediately. I have to tell you that no such undertaking has been received, and that consequently this country is at war with Germany.' This was followed by the National Anthem, the whole country stood in silence.

The Bridport Arms West Bay Dorset.

THE FISHERMEN'S REVENGE

Deep Sea Fishing Trawler

In the desperate days of World War Two at the end of May in 1940, the British Expeditionary Force in Europe was evacuated from the beaches of Dunkirk on the northern coast of France five miles from the Belgium frontier. Over 338,000 allied troops, French, Belgian, Dutch, but mostly British were brought back to the English shores by 850 ships, some as large as Royal Navy cruisers and some as small as River Thames pleasure craft. Incuded in the rescue were the S.S. St . Julien and the S.S. St. Helier passenger ships built in 1923 to carry holidaymakers from Weymouth to Jersey and Guernsey before the war, they also took part in the invasion of Normandy in 1944.

This was followed by the fall of France in June. Most of the British people felt very frustrated at the inability to strike back at the arrogant 'Hun', who now strutted over most of continental Europe. None were more aggrieved than the fishermen of the U.K. who were either too young or too old to serve in the armed forces and often they could not go to sea because of enemy action.

The Battle of Britain was at its full height in September 1940, when the fate of Great Britain was decided by 400 fighters of the Royal Air Force, the majority of which were Hurricanes, facing 4,000 German aircraft. When a fishing boat, the *Lorna Doone*, from West Bay in Dorset was attacked in the English Channel by a 'Nazi' dive-bomber. The crew managed to jump overboard before their boat sank and they were saved by another that was fishing close by.

That night the rescued crew sat drinking cider in the 'Bridport Arms' by the quay at West Bay or Bridport Harbour as the old people still call it. It was only changed to West Bay when the railways arrived in 1884. The Landlord was Lionel Robins. He was also a part-time fireman and when he was called out to a fire, galloped his white horse, which he kept in a paddock nearby, to Bridport fire station, which was a mile and a half away.

He was known as 'Uncle' Lionel, but some called him 'Tinker' after his grandfather Nathaniel 'Tinker' Robins. Now 'Nat' was a real tinker in the old days, at the end of the 19th century. Travelling Dorset, Devon and Cornwall, with his friend 'Aunt' Liza, sharpening knives, mending pots and pans, and generally fighting and thieving (but that's an other story).

Lionel was helped by his wife 'Auntie' Hilda, a dark haired beauty, blue eyes and a handsome figure, some said she was part gypsy, for if you crossed her palm with silver she would tell your fortune. Her mother Daisy Walsh was born on a farm just outside Burton Bradstock on Halloween night 1889 during a thunderstorm. It was a strange coincidence earlier that year there was a big gypsy fair up on the downs in late February. Daisy was well known for her ability to read a person's fortune in the tea leaves left in the bottom of their cups.

Although Hilda was a good-looking woman, and a real charmer, the fishermen gave her a wide berth, for it was said she could whistle up the wind if upset and the last thing a seaman wanted was a bad storm when he was at sea. On their wedding day, as the bride came down the aisle of the local church, there was a flash of lighting and an almighty crash of thunder. The organ burst into flames and the organist fell off his stool and collapsed in a heap onto the floor. The vicar the Reverend Mullard glanced at the fallen musician lying on the floor of the aisle and with a sigh, he raised his eyes to the ceiling of the church and carried on with the ceremony as if nothing had happened. The couple has now been happily married for over ten years.

The lads liked the local brewed Palmiters beer especially the I.P.A. But Cider was only four pence halfpenny (2p) a pint whilst beer was nine pence (4p), and with no fish caught and a boat lost cider was the drink this unhappy night.

Young Jimmy Westcott complained. 'I even lost me shoes, the only pair I 'ad, I borrowed these from my granny,' pointing to the old fashioned pair of black boots he was wearing.

'Why can't we have a go at them German blighters?'

'That's easier said than done,' big John Enticott grumbled into his jar of scrumpy, it was his boat the *Lorna Doone*, which he had owned for over twenty years and named after his mother Lorna, that the Jerries had sunk that fine sunny September day in 1940.

'I've lost me boat and all I own, I now be dead broke. The only thing I managed to save was my gun,' he complained. 'I always carried my 12-bore shotgun but it didn't do much good against that stukeer, did it? Gave it both barrels of deer shot too! Pity we can't lob one of them-there landmines that gets washed up on the beach at 'em.'

John was a big man over six feet tall with fair ginger hair, he was not fat but he was very strong and could lift nearly anything. His favourite saying when something went wrong was to say,

'I didn't do it!' He originally came from Broad Windsor and moved to West Bay when his father got a job with Drakes rope making company in Bridport. The foreman at the works was Sid Turner who was the best skittler in the whole of the Dorset league and many a time had scored twenty-seven pins down with only three balls. His only son Tony sang in the choir of St Mary's church in Bridport. John Enticott was now in his mid forties and married to Elsie who also worked for the rope works.

His oldest son, sixteen-year-old George was an apprentice with Westland Aircraft Company in Yeovil, he lodged with Mrs Matthews in West Hendford near the factory. Also at the house was billeted Sergeant Gordon Nichols, who was in charge of the RAF Barrage Balloon site opposite, guarding to town from low flying attacks by enemy aircraft. Nick was courting Gwen Harris, who was a lovely girl but a bit of a handful mind you, until she went off to Scotland with a sailor from Yeovilton Royal Naval Air Station, named H.M.S.Heron, when he was posted to Lossiemouth. Nick who was the RAF boxing champion would have killed him if he had caught him.

Young George Enticott was going out with Rose Trott, whom he met at the Saturday night dance held in the Hall of the Liberal Club in Yeovil. A lovely girl with ginger hair and green eyes, she had a beautiful smile and an easy laugh, George was doing quite well until her father Sid caught them in a compromising situation in the back of his Vauxhall 14 car which was new at the time. Sidney

Trott was a local glazier and a hard man and threatened to do some unspeakable things to him with some broken glass if he ever saw him again. So ended the young lads first sojourn into the hidden mysteries of courting, women and his fling with poor young Rosie.

Denzil Symmonds was 44, a real Dorset boy and a bit on the slow side but a deep thinker. He had served in the Royal Navy in the First World War and never went above the rank of stoker. Then after thinking quietly for a long time spoke up.
'Why can't we make a torpedo and fire it into one of their harbours?'
'Daft beggar,' they all said.

'But if we made a long tube or box fixed a mine on the front and a propeller to the back and aim it at the Germans, that'll make the Jerries sit up a bit,' continued Denzil.
He was always coming up with something new or some outlandish plan or mad idea, which usually got the gang into trouble, he was also a bit of a poacher on the side, so there was always rabbit pie on the menu in the pub.
They all sat quietly for a while, then Pete Hussey who was the sticker-up for the skittle team, although only 16 years old he was a smart lad, a bit of a mummy's boy but always full of bright ideas, said.
'My Uncle Frank, 'Dinky' Bugler runs a veg' shop in Bridport. He's got lots of Fyffe's wooden banana boxes at the back of his shop and as he can't get no bananas because of the war they be no good to him now, Them's about three to four foot long and eighteen inches square. If we fixed two together end to end and covered in tar and canvas to make 'em water tight they would make an ideal torpedo.'
The thoughts were now coming thick and fast. Archie Brooks, who was the Skipper of the *Mary Lou*, aged about 60, bald as a coot, with a big friendly smile and a bit of a rogue on the side now put in his suggestion.
'My Dad has an old tractor up Top Field by Eype, been in a ditch for years, we could use the radiator fan off that to propel it. The old man's well over eighty now don't expect 'e will want it again, as 'e won't last much longer anyway, for only last month 'e married a woman half is age, she's a big girl and will surely kill him '
'What a way to go,' someone said, and they all laughed at the idea.
'What about an electric motor and a couple of batteries? That'll drive it,' added Snowy White, the oldest of the group, always smart and still with full head of white hair and a small military moustache. He was a sombre man and

churchwarden of St Mary's the local parish church.

He kept a small garage in the town but with a war on and petrol rationed it was very quiet now, so he often went fishing with the boys and liked a pint and a chat with them in the evening.

He had been quite a lively lad in his younger days, a bit of a ladies man, a smart dresser and a good dancer. Then he met Dulcie the vicar's daughter who soon brought him into line.

'I'll phone my father-in-law, Jack Williams. He works at Whiteheads the torpedo works in Wyke Regis just by Ferrybridge near Weymouth. He might know a bit about it,' suggested Maxie.

'No don't do that the less that know about it the better I say,' Snowy said. He was always worried that things might come back to cause him embarrassment.

Maxie Samways, who had joined Lord Kitchener's new army in 1915 at the age of 17. With his father-in-law out of the equation, added his contribution to this crazy endeavour.

'Yeah, and fix one of them landmines to the front, push that into Roscoff Harbour on the North West coast of France. That'll shake the swines up a bit, and get our own back too.'

'But why Roscoff? ` Someone queried.

'Well now see, Cherbourg is too heavily defended with big guns and all that. Le Havre is too far and has good air cover by the German fighters and St Malo we will have to go right through the German controlled Channel Islands to get there. Now Roscoff is right out of the way to the west and not defended that much and we will get a good Westerly Wind coming home, see!' Explained Maxie, the ex-soldier and knew a lot about those sorts of things.

A week later in the corner of the same pub, the motley crew looked very glum.

'Can't get a battery anywhere,' moaned Snowy White, who not only kept a garage but had a small scrap-yard as well. 'Worth their weight gold now there's a war on. I don't know what we're gonna'do. I even tried Johnny Farr's junk-yard at Burton Bradstock but he's only got old prams, bike parts and some old motor bikes and I've been Alfie Score's scrap-yard up Chickerell way near Dorchester.'

'Farr's OK for bike bits, I made a complete bike from spares I bought from him for five bob,' said Pete Hussey. 'Cycled to Weymouth and back on it the other day.'

A long silence followed, until young Jimmy Westcott spoke up. Although he was only 16 years old he was drinking cider with the rest of the fishermen. He had crewed with them since he could walk. They were all related to him in some way or other and help bring him up as his father went away to the South Seas when his wife died of TB.

'I fly my model aeroplanes with elastic bands,' said Jimmy, a keen model-maker and although a good seaman he wanted to go into the Royal Air Force and be a fighter pilot.

Ten seconds elapsed and Big John was about to hit him across the back of his head, when Maxie who was a bit of a fixer or some said a bodger, suggested.
  'What about those elastic hawser ropes we use for the trawls? So if they get caught on a snag, like a rock or a wreck they give rather than snap. Wind them up tight like young Jimmy's aeroplanes that will do the trick '
  'That's a good idea!' They all said.

Many weeks later after hours of fixing and bodging, the torpedo was ready for testing. It was tried out on the waters of the River Brit, where the water backs up into a small lake behind the weir of West Bay harbour. A large block of concrete was tied to the front in place of the mine. It had fins made of ply-wood at the back and a ratchet fixed to the drive shaft as a brake and inside the long box was fifty feet of elastic rope fixed to a hook at the front and the propeller shaft at the rear. To begin with it floated too high in the water so they tied a row of bricks underneath to balance it. After a few trials this did the trick. The elastic was wound-up about a hundred times with the help of a starting handle from an old Austin Seven car. The contraption was held steady by two of the lads standing in the water with their waders on. Maxie pulled the lever up to release the ratchet; the propeller thrashed the water like a landed conger-eel, splashing everyone in sight.
  The two boys holding the machine fell back into the muddy water that looked like thick brown soup, gasping and spluttering and the weapon shot across the lake at a fast rate of knots heading for the opposite bank. Mrs Ada Knight, whose husband Jack was away at sea with the Royal Navy, had five daughters. Molly, Joyce, Barb, Betty and Audrey, and with all the soldiers about she was always looking for one or the other of her girls, except little Audrey who was only eight years old.
On this particular balmy autumn evening, Ada Knight she was out looking for

one of her girls. She was walking along the path by river trying to find Molly. When she had the fright of her life as this large black oblong box shot out of the water like some banshee and landed in front of her, the propeller still churning and the elastic moaning, groaning and whining. She screamed like mad, ran all the way to Bridport as if the Devil Himself was after her. She then reported the incident to Police Constable Stan Mock the local policeman, but when he cycled back to where the alleged offence had taken place there was no sign that any misdemeanour had ever happened. And with much pomp he reported as such to his superior officer, Chief Inspector Hannam, who said.

'Keep on to it Mock, we don't want any funny business in our neck of the woods, do we constable?'

'No, sir, but something funny is going on, I'm sure of that.'

The lads had long scarpered back to their boat-shed like a pack of long dogs with the contraption on a fish barrow and hid it at the back of the shed under a load of old fishing nets.

'That was a close call,' remarked Pete, worried that his mum might find out.

'But it went well didn't it?' Said Maxie. 'Did you see the beggar go? Like a bat out of Hell, shame about Ada though, bet she don't want any Epsom salts tonight. The last time I saw 'er run that fast was when Charlie Penfold's bull chased 'er round Dorchester market just after the Great War.'

'Ah, but you should have known her sister Gladys, now she were a goer,' said Snowy White, with a twinkle in his eye. He was well over 60, and although now a sombre man and went to church regularly he had been quite a boy in his younger days. 'I remember she said to me once. "You can put it in but don't let 'im squirt," he laughed as he recalled the incident of many years ago.

'Enough of that,' commented Archie. 'Lets get home smartish like, before the misses wants to know where I been to and how come I'm so wet. She been out to a W.I. meeting tonight and won't be home just yet, see you all tomorrow night to sort out the details of the attack.'

Next day, the conspirators were sat around their usual table in the corner of the pub. The plan was being worked out.

'We need a night with no moon but plenty of stars, I reckon about first week in November two weeks after Hunter's Moon will be just right,' said Archie Brooks. Who was the most experienced of all the fishermen on the south Devon and Dorset coast. He had sailed these waters in all winds and weathers for most of his sixty years except for the Great War, as had his father and grandfather before him. He knew every cove, bay and estuary in this part of the English Channel.

Everyone said that he could catch fish even when he was drunk, which he often was. He had served in the Royal Navy as an Able Seaman during the 1914-18 War with the Home Fleet.

'We'll sail out at daybreak.' he continued. 'Cross most of the Channel during the day and move in close at night-fall, let the blighter go and be home by teatime the next day.'

'But they'll hear us with our motor going and see us if we get in close even if it is dark. My mum will kill me if I get shot,' young Pete complained. A hush descended on the group and apart from a few umms and ahhs no one spoke for quite a while. Then Big John, who was a bit of a thinker, suggested. 'What about that pedalo at the back of the boat shed called the *Mickey Mouse*. It's no use to anyone now the beach is being covered with iron poles to stop the German invasion. We could lash the torpedo to that, have it on the deck of the trawler, get to about a mile or less from the target and lift it over the side with the derrick. Then two of us peddle it to about four hundred yards from the shore let'n go, then back to the ship sharpish like and head for home.'
They had a few drinks by now and the sheer audacity or stupidity of the scheme it seamed a good idea at the time but left some speechless.
'Well has anyone a better ideal?' he muttered. 'Let's vote on it.'
Young Pete was worried. 'Uncle Dinky will tell my mum and she won't let me ever go fishing ever again,' he commented, shaking his head and looking down at the floor.
'I vote we leave young Pete ashore as watch-dog and go ahead according to Big John's plan,' said Archie, anxious to make a decision and get home.' But what if someone bangs the mine before we get there, won't it go off?' Asked Jimmy.
'No,' explained Max. 'We'll cover it with a Huntley & Palmer's biscuit tin, that's about the right size and take it off just before we let'n go. Let's vote and get on with it.' He was now getting fed-up with all the argie-bargie.

The cider was now having quite an effect, for they all were agreed whole heartedly with the new plan and the date was set for about two weeks time on a day when the weather looked right. Then they all left the pub and made their merry way home, singing as they went.
'Roll out the barrel, let's have a barrel of fun.'

Twelve days later they were huddled in the corner of their local pub.

'OK,' said Archie. 'Tomorrow we go, the weather will be just right, a bit cloudy during the day, a clear night and a nice westerly wind to see us home, it'll be ideal. Every body set?'

The bravado of two weeks ago had somewhat evaporated that evening in the pub, with a few looking very doubtful and sheepish, but four pints of cider later, topped up with a couple of navy rums from Archie's hip flask they were raring to go.

In the cold light of dawn the next day, with all the crew nursing a mighty hangover the *Mary Lou* sailed out of West Bay harbour on it's covert mission. The secret weapon was on the deck of the trawler covered by a large tarpaulin and some fishing nets. In the early mist they were watched by the disappointed but much relived Pete Hussey, and a couple of soldiers on duty at the end of the pier, smoking a crafty fag took no notice of the coming and going of the local fishermen. The only other people about that time of the morning was Mrs Kelly sweeping sand from the step of her newspaper kiosk on the front, as she waited for the papers to be delivered and Mary Korput who had a small café next door.

The Kelly family originally came from Ireland just after the 14-18 War, to work in the new flax factory in Yeovil. This was a Government scheme to relieve unemployment and to produce linen in England but because of cheap imports from India and Egypt this failed. The factory closed and Mrs Kelly took over the small kiosk on the front of West Bay while her husband was away in the regular army

Mrs Korput ran the small café on the front serving tea and cakes. Mary was born in Cornwall and was from an old Cornish family, the Lawrys. She still had many relatives in the old Duchy and on the Isles of Scilly, especially on the isle of Tresco where old granny Lawry lived and had never been of the island. Mary joined the W.A.A.F.'S (Woman's Auxiliary Air Force,) and was stationed at RAF Warmwell in Dorset; this was one of the front line Battle of Britain airfields. Mary was one of the parachute packers when she met and married a Polish pilot called Jan. Mary left the RAF when her baby Roger was born. Jan Korput had been a pilot in the Polish Air Force and when the German armies invaded his country in 1939. He escaped to England by flying his plane to Sweden and being smuggled on a British boat to Yarmouth. Jan joined the RAF and had the unique distinction of shooting down one of the first German bombers of the war, a Heinkel 111 over Portland Harbour. His father, although Polish, he had served as a bodyguard for Nicholas 11 the Russian tsar, who didn't trust his own people. He fought the Germans as a Calvary officer in the First World War and after the 1917 revolution returned Poland and joined the Polish Air Force.

Jan still had many relatives in that Nazi occupied country.

The large fishing vessel negotiated the narrow harbour entrances and out into the open sea. The seagulls were soaring and swooping overhead, making lots of noise with their screeching and calling, hoping for some fish or scraps from the boat.

'Why do they always sound as if they laughing?' Someone commented.

'I don't know,' said Snowy, 'but I reckon they're laughing at us, we must be blooming mad, I 'aint drinking with you lot ever again.'

On the side of the long black device on the deck of the ship was painted in white lettering.

TO ADOLF FROM THE DORSET FISHERMEN.

Denzil gave the biscuit tin a good slap and said. 'That'll shake the blighters.'

'Don't do that,' they all shouted. 'It might go off.'

'No it won't, it will take more than that,' he said. But young Jimmy was about to jump overboard, the rest of the crew went very pale and Snowy was sick over the side of the boat. It was a chilly misty day with a bit of low cloud and the smell of salt and seaweed in the air. 'I'm starving,' moaned Jimmy.

'You've got a long gut,' Denzil said. 'You's always hungry, get out the frying pan and the Primus stove and fry them eggs and bacon, so we can 'ave our breakfast.'

Half an hour later they were tucking into a hearty meal accompanied by hunks of bread and mugs of strong tea laced with Nestlé's condensed milk and a dash of rum.

'It's like the Last Supper,' Snowy moaned.

'Oh, shut up, you're a right old Jonah,' said Max.

'I don't know how you gets so much bacon, Archie?' Someone queried.

'Well now see, the local Butcher's wife, Freda Leach, she likes a bit of fish sometimes, so I gives her the fish and I gets a bit of bacon, see,' he said with a smirk.

'That's not all you gets,' some one said and they all laughed.

'What's for tea?' Asked Jimmy.

'Pilchard sandwiches,' said Archie.

'I hate tin pilchards, especially in tomato sauce, me auntie Doris used to give us them for Sunday tea when we went to see her,' moaned Jimmy.

'You'll eat them when the time comes,' they all said.

With a light breeze the *Mary Lou* chugged all day southwest and during the trip the crew took it in turns to wind up the elastic until it was really tight. As it got dark the sky cleared and the stars came out. It was a fine clear night with a light breeze. Archie checked the sky and said. 'We're dead on course and about the right time too. Let's 'ave a mug of cocoa with a dash of Archie's rum in it.'

'I'd like to know how 'e gets so much rum now there's a war on? Hope he's not been sniffing around Auntie Hilda or we're all in trouble, and that's for sure,' someone said.

At exactly ten o'clock Archie looked at the sky again. 'This will do,' he said and stopped the trawler's engine. It was very quiet apart from the water gently splashing on the side of the boat and the quiet murmur of the sea. They could just make out the French coast in the distance, not a light to be seen anywhere. It was deadly quiet. Snowy long sorrowful face was paler than ever.

'Come on then, let's get this operation over with,' said Archie.

The small pedalo was lowered over the side of the ship, Big John and Denzil got into their attack vessel and cast-off. It wallowed a great deal in the open sea and Denzil nearly went over the side and would have been lost if Big John hadn't grabbed his jacket and pulled him back in.

'Blooming hell,' he shouted, 'I nearly went in and I can't swim.'

'Shush, the Germans will hear you if you don't shut up, now start pedalling and get this thing going, so we can get home as soon as we can,' said Big John.

Off they went pedalling and splashing their way towards the enemy coast. It took longer than they had anticipated even on a calm night like this but within half an hour they were about four hundred yards from the harbour entrance.

They lined the projectile up onto the target and undid the lashings.

'Let'n go then,' ordered Denzil. 'Don't forget to take off the biscuit tin.'

Big John took off the cover and pulled up the lever to release the ratchet. Perhaps because of the damp or the fact the elastic was wound so tight the propeller went quite slow at first but within a few seconds it went off like a rocket, heading for the enemy and on its mission of destruction.

'Blooming heck,' yelled Denzil, 'let's get out of here quick.'

They turned their pleasure craft around and headed back to the trawler pedalling like mad. They were over half way back when an almighty bang came from the shore and all hell was let loose, with big guns going off, machine guns and small arms firing in all directions.

'Hell,' yelled Denzil, 'get back to the ship and out of here or we be dead ducks.'

Archie brought his ship towards the daring duo and they scrambled aboard the safety of their main craft leaving The *Mickey Mouse* to his own devises. Captain Brooks of the *Mary Lou* turned his ship about gave her full throttle and headed for home and they hoped safety. Just then a large searchlight began to sweep the sea and coming in their direction.

'Quick, get them smoke barrels over the side,' ordered Archie.

They had brought with them three large barrels with pebbles in the bottom to balance them, then a layer of wood shavings then tarred cloth and rope and touch hole in the side to light the devise.

Careful not to show a light, Denzil put a match through the holes and soon black smoke began to pour out of the top of the barrels. Putting a bung into the each hole to keep the water out, the black belching smoke screens were lifted over the side of the ship and into the water.

'My Gawd,' spluttered Archie, coughing and choking. 'Reminds me of the old *Hood.*'

'What, the one the *Bismark* sunk? ' Asked Jimmy.

'No, the old *Hood*, a cruiser from before the First World War. She were an old coal fired, took two days to coal her up from colliers along side in Pompey harbour, but only one day in Hong Kong or Singers with the Chinese coolies out there. With a bit of rough coal she smoked like hell, worse than my old Dad's pipe when 'e were smoking Players Navy cut plug tobacco, she were scuttled by the Royal Navy in the South entrance of Portland harbour in 1939 to stop Jerry submarines entering the harbour and firing torpedoes into the moorings.'

The searchlight from the shore now swung their way and hit the great clouds of black smoke that hid them from the enemy. This must have puzzled the Germans, for apart from a few stray shots they ignored the large cloudbank and the daring commandos went on their merry way home.

The first thing they did was to open a bottle of the best Navy rum and all-hands had a large slurp to calm their nerves and to celebrate the success of the operation.

'Ah, a nice bit of Pusser's straight out of Portland docks,' said Archie.

'You'll get caught, my lad, one of these fine days,' muttered Big John, shaking his head.

'No, them Navy Officers likes their lobsters and crabs too much for that,' chuckled the skipper.

They were all laughing and giggling now that the tension was over, slapping each other on the back.

Young Jimmy Westcott dancing the sailors hornpipe on the top of the cabin and some of the crew singing 'Yo ho ho and a bottle of rum', as they raised a Jolly Roger flag from the masthead. The wind freshened and with trawl-sail up and the engine going flat out they made good time.

By dawn were over halfway home, the sky was overcast, low clouds were scurrying overhead and a good westerly wind behind them, and they were very pleased with themselves and the success of the operation. During the day they heard the noise of a few aircraft overhead, which worried them a bit.

Snowy said. 'They be looking for us, they be. If Luftwaffe see us we be in for another strafing.'

'O shut up you old Jonah, the low clouds will cover us,' Archie said with confidence.

On the way back they put out the fishing lines and reeled in hundreds of mackerel.

'No sense in wasting the trip,' said Archie.

'Let's fry some now and have our tea, I'm hungry,' complained Jimmy.

'Not again!' They all shouted.

By four o'clock they were five miles from home, the sky was clearing and nothing was more heartening than the sight of 'Golden Cap' the highest point on the South Coast glowing in the sunset.

Just then Jimmy shouts. 'Look out! There's a mine dead-ahead!'

Archie puts the tiller hard over and Big John fended the dangerous weapon off with a boat hook, avoiding the deadly horns. Slowly the evil device was pushed along the side of the boat and out of harms way. When it was about thirty yards away Big John fired his 12 bore gun at it and after the second shot it blew up with an almighty boom covering the boat and crew with spray

'My God,' moaned Snowy, 'my 'eart won't stand much more of this. Quick, give me another slug of that rum.'

The danger now over, the trawler approached West Bay harbour. The crew was surprised to see the pier crowded with people, many cheering and clapping. Although they had kept the operation secret, some one had said some thing and it had gone around the local population like a bush fire.

'Now we're in trouble and that's for sure, I can see my misses in the crowd,' moaned Archie. Vera Brooks was a formidable woman, one of the Curtis girls from Weymouth, a Baptist Sunday-school teacher, also the chairwoman of the local W.I. She stood on the quayside with her arms folded across her ample bosom and Archie knew he was in for a lot of tongue-pie.

They tied-up alongside the quay and started to unload their catch. When Captain C.O.Jones M.C. of the local militia arrived. (Know as cojones by some, which means something in Spanish). Puffed up with his own importance. Sergeant Neil McNeil followed him with two more soldiers of the Queens Own Cameron Highlanders and P.C. Stanley Wilberforce Mock, the local Constable.

'I want to know exactly where you have been and what were your duties?' Enquired the officer.

'Been fishing, sir,' answered Archie. Not a man to say too much when then there may be trouble about.

'I want to see the ships log!' Demanded Captain Jones.

'Ain't got no log, sir,' Archie answered shaking his head.

'WHAT!' Cried the army officer, going from red to purple and back to red.

'You well know that the Maritime Act of 1939 section 24(a) states that. "All owners of sea going vessels over one ton in weight, must at all times record their exact position in the ships log every hour when at sea." That is the law.'

'Well, now see sir, I can't read nor write, so I've got a problem to keep a log,' responded Archie.

'Now when I was with Lord Jellicoe; then known as Sir John, on the *Iron Duke* at the Battle of Jutland in 1916 when our Grand Fleet beat the German High Sea's Fleet, it didn't seem to matter to him then when I was passing up the ammunition. And when me Great Granddad was with 'Oratio Nelson on the 100 gun *Victory* at Trafalgar on the 21st of October in 1805 it was no bother.

AND! I'd an ancestor with Sir Francis Drake when we fought the Spanish Armada 1588, not only could he not read nor write, but him being a Devon boy he couldn't even speak English proper like we do now.'

C.O.Jones went straight from purple to white. Turned on his heels and shouted to the soldiers.

'Sergeant, take that man's name!' And marched away with as much dignity as his five foot two frame could muster. The non-commissioned officer who knew the man's name anyway, said in a strong Scottish accent.

'Squad, shun, right turn, quick march, left right, left right,' and disappeared around the corner.

Archie's wife, with a look that could freeze fish said. ' Right, YOU... HOME... NOW!'

With his head down but a smile on his face mumbled, 'yes dear,' and sloped away and as he passed his mates whispered, 'see you later, lads.'

That night in the pub the tale was told over the over again. 'Did you see 'im go? -Thought we 'ad it. - I nearly went in.- what a bang. - All them guns- I was glad to be home. -My missus gave me hell. - Good though wun'it-Ain't doing that again,' they were all clamouring.

'I never prayed so much in my life,' said Snowy.

'Captain Jones was mad as hell,' said Jock.

'Most action he's ever seen in his life.' Someone commented.

'But he won the Military Cross in the First World War, didn't he?' Pete asked.

'Yes,' said Snowy, 'he was a second Lieutenant stationed at headquarters in Paris. Went for a horse ride one day, got lost behind the enemy lines, drooped his blooming gun and shot a German soldier by mistake. Lost his horse and was rescued by a French taxi driver. Made up to a captain and sent home a flipping hero. A rousing chorus of. 'For he's a jolly fine fellow, he's no blooming good to any one, he's no blooming good at all,' was sung with much gusto by all.

The Scottish boys were really enjoying themselves, drinking cider, whisky and then more cider, until the pub ran dry. The highlanders had escaped from Dunkirk at the end of May, Some said they floated out to rescue ships on their bagpipes.

They came back to England with all their gear, tin hats, rifles and even their gas masks although they were the last to leave the beaches, having to fight a rear-guard action right across Belgium.

They were now part of the defence of the U.K. especially to repel any invasion in the Lyme Bay area.

'Aye, you should have seen the 'Boche' freeze and quake at the sound of the pipes,' said Jock Fraser, recounting their time in Flanders. The sergeant added. 'It was not the so much the pipes but when we ran out of bullets we had eighteen inches of cold steel on the end of our rifles, och they don't like that up 'um and that's a fact.'

All was quiet for several weeks, Captain Jones wrote his report, the Chief Inspector and his Police Constable kept a weather eye on the mischief-makers. And their wives made sure no one got up to anything.

A month after the escapade, Archie had a call to go the big House; he often went there with fish etc. for the local squire Major Sir John Farquhar-Smythe J.P. M.C. D.S.O. and Bar. He knocked on the door of the kitchen, as was his usual custom.

The cook Mrs Marsh opened the door and gave him a friendly smile, for she had a soft spot for the weather-beaten old rogue.

''Ello Archie,' said Mabel.' 'Ow nice to see you again, ain't seen 'e for a bit. Must come up some time for a chat, a cup of tea and a piece of cake, like you used to do,' she said with a cheeky grin.

'Now the Master would like see you in his study,' she added.

Now this worried Archie, the only time he ever went into the inner sanctum was at Christmas time when he was given a brace of pheasants and a bottle of port, for all he had done during the year.

James the butler showed the fisherman into Sir John's large library.

'Mr Brooks, Sir,' he announced as he bowed, left the room and closed the door. Archie looked around the room, with its hundreds of books, antique furniture, ancient weapons on the wall and a wood fire burning in the open hearth. The Squire was sat in a large leather chair by the fire.

'Take your coat off Brooks and sit down. A small whisky?' Handing Archie a large cut-glass goblet with about a eighth of a bottle of the best highland malt in it. 'I do hope you and your good lady are well, and looking forward to Christmas? Must be awfully nice not to have to go fishing for a few days.'

'Thank you Sir John,' stammered the old sea salt, screwing up his cap in his hand. Such a thing had never happened to him before. 'I brought you a nice turbot, Sir John, a couple of big crabs and some mackerel for the cats.' Trying not to bow and scrape too much, for it wasn't in his nature but he was a bit worried.

'Thank you Brooks; very kind I'm sure. Lady Dorothy always looks forward to some nice fresh fish. Now you may not know but my brother Giles works at the War Office in London, secret job, M.I. something or other. He gave me a call last weekend; some do in France by all accounts. It seems some fishermen chaps from the south coast pushed an explosive device into Roscoff harbour went up the slipway across the road and hit the wall of Chateaubriand Cafe. Injuring four

German soldiers who were inside drinking wine and playing cards. Also the French waiter Maurice was hit by flying glass, luckily the owner Jean-Paul saved from harm by the large oak counter that he was standing behind.

None the less he is very upset as two bottles of pastis, a bottle of calvados and three very good bottles of Claret fell onto the flagstone floor and were smashed. He now threatens to sue the British Government for the cost.' The Squire let the words sink in for a while; then said. 'Now, you know a few of the locals chaps, don't you Archie?' Using his Christian name for the first time ever. 'Will you put the word about, as we don't want this sort of cavalier action going on, do we?' Archie was now feeling very hot, it was a warm day or it may have been the fire or the whisky but he was sweating well.

'No sir, I mean yes sir,' stammering and spluttering. 'I'll, I'll see what I- I can do sir.' He managed to stutter. Drinking up his whisky with a gulp.

'Jolly good,' said the Squire; ' we'll leave it at that then shall we, what?'

The squire pressed the bell by his large leather chair and the butler appeared immediately.

'Yes Sir John?' He said to his Master, giving Archie a broad smile and a sly wink. The Squire rose and Archie jumped to his feet grabbing his hat and coat, now very keen to leave.

'James, will you please see the gentleman out.'

As they went across the hall to the front door, which the butler opened, the Magistrate for South Dorset put his arm around the fisherman's shoulder and said.

'Jolly good show, what? Awfully well done, but leave it to the experts next time, will you?'

A week later two free firkins of Palmiter's best bitter and a hogshead of Director's Strong ale was delivered to the pub for the fishermen to sample. Which was done with much merry making. To add to the occasion Archie had two bottles of Pusser's rum and the Scottish lads had some whisky sent down from home. Auntie Hilda provided plates of faggots, peas and mashed potato, some pig's trotters, local blue vinnie cheese with large chunks of cottage loaf bread and home made pickled onions.

The celebration was fantastic and went on long into the night and even Vera Brooks had a good time and after a few sherries was standing by the piano giving a fantastic rendition of the WI anthem *Jerusalem*. A good time was had by all, and so ended this marvellous episode of the Dorset fishermen.

(For those unfamiliar with local words perhaps a slight explanation will help.

Pompey and Singers is naval slang for Portsmouth and Singapore. Faggots are meatballs made with liver onions and bread. Pusser's is navy issue rum, firkins and hogsheads are sizes of beer barrels, scrumpy was strong local cider, Epson salts were a laxative and Jerries were Germans.)

This story is a folk legend of South Dorset as told to me by my Great Uncle Lionel just before he died, with these words. *'They also served who only went to sea and fished.'*

East Cliff and Harbour entrance West Bay 1939

THE BEST DRINK IN THE WEST

All was quiet for a long time in the sleepy backwaters of West Bay, until one night in the 'Bridport Arms', Issy Isaccs was moaning and groaning to the lads who were sat around a table in corner of the bar drinking their beer and eating some bread and cheese with a few pickled onions. Now Issy had a farm up by Seatown, not so much a farm more like a small holding, half a dozen pigs, four cows, twenty chickens and a few ducks. He grew a few potatoes but his main interest was cider, or scrumpy as it was called.

He had a large orchard with all sorts of apples, you name them he grew them, Kingston Black, Dabinett, Stoke Red, Yarlington Mill, Tremlett's Bitter, Dorset crabs, Taylor's Sweet and many more. They all said he made the best cider in Dorset or even the World, but then to some Dorset was the whole World. It was made in the traditional way, chopping up the apples perhaps the odd carrot and parsnip using an old rusty iron machine with a big wooden handle, then putting layers of straw then layers of apples to form a big heap, called a cheese, into a large wooded press. A long pole harnessed to an old donkey called Ned, who went and round a round the press turning the screw and squashing the pile.

Before the war Issy used to take Ned to the beach and give rides to the children for a penny a go. Issy and the donkey wore old trilby hats to keep off the sun and with their long sorrowful faces it was a very hard job to tell them apart.

The juice ran into a stone gully to a massive wooden vat and everyone was sure some of Ned's droppings went in as well. Added to this went some bacon bones, a horseshoe for luck and they say a couple of dead rats for good measure. When it had finished fermenting, the bones, horseshoe and all had dissolved. It was light golden in colour a bit cloudy but it tasted good and was very strong; it wasn't called tangle-foot or cripple-cock for nothing. It was best mixed with something like lemonade or Vimto to ease the strength a bit. The traditional cider jug had two handles to stop your hand shaking too much and spilling the contents.

The left over from the press was fed to the pigs and was a marvellous sight to behold to see them rolling around the yard, drunk as handcarts. It was the best laugh around but that was before T.V.

'What's up Issy? You looks like you's lost half-a-crown and found sixpence,' said Denzil.

'Well, it's like this, you see,' he explained. 'I had some fish meal delivered t'other day, they said it makes good fertiliser for the tomatoes and I put it in the shed next to the cider vat to keep it dry like. But the smell has got into the cider and it tastes horrible, real fishy like and no one will drink it, not even the squaddies up at the camp. I don't know what to do with it'.

'That's a terrible shame, I don't know the answer to that,' said Snowy, who knew the answer to most things, him being a Grammar School boy who had gone to Waddam's in Crewkerne.

'Well I don't want to throw it away, that would be a wicked waste,' he moaned. All went quiet for a long time as they sat drinking their beer and thinking. Then like a bolt from the blue, Archie sat upright like he had been stung by a wasp and said with a broad smile on his face.

'I've just been up to Alfie Score's scrap-yard, looking around for a few bits and pieces for the boat. In the corner of the yard was a load of stuff from the Weymouth Brewery that was bombed last month. Boilers, pipes, tubes and things. I said to Alfie, what's that cooper coil for then? He said it's a still for making alcohol.'

'Well, so what? That won't help Issy, will it?' Jimmy asked.

'But don't you see if we put his cider though a still it will make some sort of hooch. When I used to go over to France before the war, taking lobsters for the fancy restaurants in Paris and bringing back the French onion Jonnies with their bikes, I used to drink that Calvados, it was a type of brandy distilled from cider. Ever so fiery and very strong but it did you a power of good.'

'But that's illegal!' Exploded Snowy.

'So's everything else these days, you can't do anything with out breaking some rule or regulation. It's either immoral, illegal or it makes you fart,' complained Big John.

'But we don't know anything about distilling, how are we going to do it?' Asked Denzil.

'We could ask one of the Scottish soldiers we drink with, they're always in here,' suggested John.

'They're no good, two worked in the ship building yard in Glasgow and the other was a coal miner,' explained Archie.

'There's that old Scottish chap, Willy Henderson that drinks up at the 'Hope and Anchor' in Bridport, I heard he used to work in one of those places that make whisky up in the Highlands of Scotland, he may know a thing or two about it.'

'We will have to very careful, we don't want to let on what we're doing or we will be in trouble again,' said Snowy. Looking more worried than usual and shaking his head, remembering the last time with the torpedo. He reckoned his hair went even whiter then than before.

'Don't worry so much Snowy. We'll get Big John to suss him out, every one trusts him,' said Archie.

Later on in the week the lads got out one their rowing boats and went up the river to Bridport and the 'Hope and Anchor', owned by Fred Pearce.

It was that or walk and as Archie said it was safer to row down river than walk when you've had a few beers, better to drown than be knocked down by an army lorry.

'There he is, in the corner. Go on John, speak to him,' said Archie.

'Don't rush, you got to take these things steady,' Big John replied. 'Get a drink in first, I'll have a cider, I'm thirsty with all that rowing.'

'Hello, Willy, how you doing, fancy a drink?' Asked Big John.

'Good day to you John. I'll have a wee whisky if you don't mind. They should have some in stock being Thursday; the squaddies don't get paid till tomorrow. By the way what's the occasion? You don't usually go splashing you money around.'

'Well it's just that some of the lads were wondering how whisky was made and we thought you might know.'

'It's fairly easy you know, but you don't want to go mucking about with that, it's illegal ye ken. The Revenue man don't like people doing it unless they're licensed and you could get sent to prison if you're caught.'

'Oh no, nothing like that. We was just wondering like see, just as a matter of interest,' said Big John, with a big smile and his innocent blues eyes open wide.

'Well what you do is to make a mash out of grain, barley or wheat, add some yeast and let it ferment for a while then heat it slow in a closed container and let the vapour condense through a copper coil into a large glass jar. That's how the Irish make that poteen rubbish out of potatoes. If it gets too hot you'll get steam off and that's not good, it needs to be about 210 degrees Fahrenheit. Also the first cut that comes off is poison. You don't want to drink that, first it'll make you blind, then mad and then dead.'

'Blimey,' said Big John, going a bit pale. 'What do they do with that bit then?'

'Well that's called industrial alcohol; it's what they put on your arm when you have an injection. It's like methylated spirit, they put that colour in and give it a horrible taste to stop you drinking it but that don't stop some of them alcoholics and it kills them. You can add a bit to the petrol to give that wartime rubbish a bit of a kick but not too much or it will burn your engine out. The pre-war racing drivers used to use it to give their cars more power. The raw spirit is white so they then put it in old sherry barrels for five years or more to mature it and to give it the colour and flavour. The gin people pass the stuff through charcoal filters to take out all the impurities then add a some herbs and spices, I understand some of the home-brewers pour it through their gas-mask filters and that does the trick.'

'Thanks Willy, I just wondered, I'll get that whisky for you,' said Big John.

'Thanks a lot, your O.K. John, and if you do manage to make some don't forget old Jock.'

Big John sauntered back to his mates, who were stood around the bar, supping their cider, chatting away as usual, pulling each others legs and telling usual stories, the ones they had told many times in the past but they still laughed.

'Well, what did he say?' Asked Denzil.

'Shush, not now I'll tell 'e later, when it's quiet, but it were very good and I think we have a chance.'

The group of reprobates left the pub and went on their merry way, singing as they got into their boat and paddled their way home. 'Show me the way to go home. It's a long way to tickle Mary and there's an Old mill by the stream Nellie Dean.'

Luckily no one fell into the water and they got home safe, if not sober.

Next day, they were all gathered around the boats in West Bay harbour, discussing the new project.

'I reckon it's a goer, all we need is the bits and pieces from Alfies yard, put it all together up at Issy's farm and we're in business,' enthused Archie.

'What about Issy, he may not be too keen on the scheme,' queried Snowy.

'He'll be alright, once he sees a profit in it,' stated Archie.

The lads worked hard to get the still going and were soon producing a fairly good spirit, having passed the brew though quite a lot of gas-masks filters, adding a bit of ginger and a few wild herbs and berries to give it flavour. It sold well to the soldiers for ten bob a pint, Issy was very pleased and Snowy's car certainly went better on the new mix.

It was going so well that they were even buying extra cider from Stan Derryman who had a farm at Chideock, a few miles away, to put through the still to make more of their jungle juice.

But as all good things must come to an end. They left the still one evening, bubbling away on its own while they went for a drink down the 'Anchor' pub at Seatown. They sat drinking and enjoying themselves as usual laughing and joking. But the machine they had left must have had a will of it's own.

It started to over heat, the coil became jammed up with muck, pressure built up and the whole apparatus blew up with a massive bang, smoke, flames and debris rising into the night sky. The explosion was heard as far away as Broadwinsor, a bit of the apparatus was even found on the beach at Eype over a mile away.

'My God, what was that,' everyone exclaimed in the pub. But the conspirators had a good idea what had happened. Everyone rushed outside and saw a large glow in the sky above Issy's farm.

'Oh my God, a bomb's hit the farm, my poor pigs,' cried Issy, thinking quickly. They hurried up to the farm but 'Uncle' Lionel was there first, on his white horse with his brass helmet on his head. He jumped off his horse and started to tackle the blaze with a bucket of water and a stirrup pump.

'Leave that, save the pigs and the cows, don't forget my Ned,' shouted Issy.

'Must have been some bomb,' someone said.

'A thousand pounder at lest, I recon,' said another.

'Can I get compensation?' Asked Issy, hopefully.

The fire brigade, soldiers from the camp with the C.O.Jones, an army bomb disposal squad, P.C. Mock and dozens of people from the surrounding area soon turned up to see the fun.

The damage was so bad that the authorities never could find the real cause of the explosion, so the five miscreants were let off the hook but all the gear for making the hooch was lost.

'What a blooming shame, all that stuff lost and we were doing so well,' moaned Denzil.

'We was making a bit of money, too. The Squire will be upset, he quite liked it, said it reminded him of his time in Normandy during the First World War, and he was willing to pay fifteen bob a bottle for it,' said Archie grimly.

'The Vicar liked it until I told him it was illegal, then he wouldn't buy any more unless it was mixed with Elderberries and I called it Communion wine,' murmured Snowy.

'I soaked sloe berries in it with some sugar,' said Archie. 'Mrs Brooks was quite partial to that as a nightcap it certainly made her sleep well, she said it did her back the world of good'

'Ah well, that's over then, we'll have to think of something else,' Big John stated.

'It's all right for you lot,' Issy protested. 'I've lost a barn, me ciders gone, me hens have stopped laying, me cows are only providing half the milk and one of me pigs is missing.'

'You'll be alright, you'll put a claim in for twice the amount including a new tractor and make a profit on deal,' replied Archie. 'Mrs Brooks says I've got to give up drinking and that's dam hard at my age, I dam well tell 'e, and she found out about Mabel Marsh as well, talk about trouble.'

'It were good though, weren't it, best bonfire we ever had,' remarked Jimmy laughingly. 'Flames, explosions, bangs and twelve bore cartridges going off, it were good, just like Guy Fawkes Night before the war.'

'Oh shut up, Jimmy, my wife gave me hell when she found out I was involved with you lot again,' groaned Snowy. 'I had to sleep in the spare room for a week.'

So ended another saga of the West Bay fishermen.

THE TANK

'We will fight them on the beaches in the fields and in the ditches we will never surrender.'
Winston Churchill. 1940

'What's up Archie?' Asked 'Uncle' Lionel, the landlord of the 'Bridport Arms', from behind the bar. 'You look really down in the dumps, has the missus left you?'

'No such luck, it's worse than that, can't go fishing now the army have stopped us from going to sea until this invasion scare is over. They reckon the Germans might come in disguised as fishing boats, what a load of cods-wallop. Them government chaps be off their heads,' moaned the old fisherman.

'It's the same for all of us,' said Big John. 'All I can get is a few jobs up at the camp to earn a couple of bob for a beer, pity about the brandy distilling, that was a good little earner and a good drink too.'

'I'm worried that if the Germans really do come what's to stop them. The army's no good, a lot of old has-beens now that the Jocks have left to defend Plymouth and as for the Home-Guard a few young kids and old men with broom-handles with a knife tied on the end,' commented Snowy, his face more mournful than ever.

'Not even a tank between the lot of them, they've all been withdrawn to guard Yeovil,'

'We ought to make one,' suggested Jimmy, always one for a bright idea.

'How you going to do that then, out of elastic bands, a tin box and a bit of string?' Said Denzil being a bit sarcastic. He wasn't a happy chappy these days, running short of fags and beer.

'Well up at Alfie Score's yard there's a wreck of a bren-gun carrier. He bought it off a couple of squaddies for a quid and a gallon of cider. They rolled it over up on White Hill by Abbotsbury a couple of months ago. It's got no engine or gun but we could use the body and the tracks,' Jimmy said hopefully.

'It's a bit small for a tank, we need something bigger than that to fight the Germans,' said Maxie Samways the ex-soldier.

'What about that wreck Scammell truck at the bottom of Chideock Hill. It was a funfair lorry coming down the hill when the brakes failed, crashed thought the hedge and tuned over. The trailer it was towing tore off the back and they took the engine away for spares. But if we fixed the front and the chassis to the bren-gun carrier it would be like one of those halftracks the Germans and the Americans have,' Denzil Symmonds suggested.

'It will take a bit of fixing, but I reckon we can do it,' said Maxie the bodger.

'We need an engine for it,' piped up Pete Hussey.

'That'll be hard, most things have gone for scrap,' moaned Snowy.

'There was a shot-down German Dornier on the beach but its been washed over by the sea twice a day and it's guarded by soldiers. Some one said it's got some sort of secret radio on board to help it find the target,' Archie commented.

'And the Spitfire that crashed on Golden Cap was soon whisked away by the RAF. The Merlin V Twelve Rolls Royce engine would have been ideal,' said Pete Hussey. 'It's the best engine in the world. Designed for the Schneider Trophy race.'

'What we go'na do about it then,' said Jimmy Westcott.

'What about a steam engine? We don't need petrol for them and they're very powerful,' Big John suggested.

'Don't be so stupid, where are we going to get one of them?' Asked Denzil

'There's an old White's steam lorry in Palmiters Brewery yard; they used to deliver the beer with it during the First World War. The back axle's broke and the tyres have gone but the engine is still there. I think we could use that,' suggested Archie.

'You could ask Mr. Palmiter, Snowy, you both being Freemasons.'

'You're not one of them funny hand-shake people are you?' Ask Jimmy.

'Enough of that, those things are private and we don't like to talk about it. Anyway we don't like to take advantage of it,' Snowy said grumpily.

'There is no harm in asking, we do need it for the war effort and the defence of Bridport and England,' commented Archie.

'I'll see what I can do,' said Snowy

Two days later in their local pub.

'Mr. Palmiter said we can have the steam truck but we've got to take it all away and leave no mess,' stated Snowy. 'He is a very good man and wants to do his bit for the country.'

'Right then, tomorrow we all go up to the brewery and collect the machinery for the project,' ordered Big John.

After a week of much sawing, hammering, bolting and welding, the bren-gun carrier, the lorry parts and the steam engine came together into one whole giant war-machine.

'It looks great, just like one of those German halftracks you see on the newsreels.'

'Even better,' commented the two young boys.

'Needs a gun, it's not much good without a gun. Unless the boiler blows up and kills a few Jerries,' Snowy stated.

'What about that old World War howitzer, that was captured from the Germans in 1918 in the square at Beaminster. No one will miss that, it will be just right,' Denzil suggested.

'How are we going to get that then?' Asked John.

'We get a bit of official looking paper, write the proper words on it signed proper like. Then I'll put my harbour master's suit on, the two lads wear their ATC uniform, Snowy with his best dark suit and bowler hat and we'll grab a couple of them home guard chaps then we'll go and collect it, OK?' Said Archie.

Next day they duly went to the small town of Beaminster, six miles north of Bridport. There in the main square was the gun on a concrete plinth.

'Right you lads, it's a bit heavy to load onto Snowy's truck so we will have to tow it. Squirt some oil into the axles and fix it to the back of the truck,' ordered Archie. Just then several people appeared including the local postmaster.

'What are you people doing here?' He asked.

'This gun is being requisitioned for the defence of Bridport,' stated Archie with a smart naval salute and handing the enquirer the appropriate piece of paper.

The German military 1918, 4 inch Howitzer situated in the Square of the Town of Beaminster in the County of Dorsetshire.

"To Whom It May Concern:

The bearers of this document are hereby authorized to remove the aforesaid military weapon and take it to the Town of Bridport, for the defence of the South Coast against the possibility of an enemy invasion."

W.Churchill

The first day of Marsh 1941. High Admiral of the Lyme Bay Auxiliary Fleet.

The gathered people duly inspected the impressive looking document with its important signature.

'Well it seems OK to me. And it looks like the Prime Minister signed it. But I don't like it, that gun's been here since the Great War, it's part of the town,' grumbled the postmaster. 'But if it is for the defence of the realm we can't object can we? But we want it back when the war is over, you make sure of that.'

'When it's no longer required we'll bring it straight back,' assured Archie, with another salute.

With that the prized weapon was towed back to Snowy's yard creaking and groaning every yard of the way. The next day was spent in taking apart and cleaning the gun. The barrel was then fixed on top of one of the wheels with the axle welded to the floor of the brengun carrier so that it would swivel.

'It can only move sideways or backwards. If we fire it to the front the shells will hit the cab,' said Denzil.

'That will do me. If the Germans come you can fire it backwards 'cause I'll be going north as fast as it will go,' said Big John.

'What are we going to do about ammunition? We need something to fire or the whole thing is blooming useless,' Jimmy stating the obvious.

'I thought about that,' said Archie. 'In Alfie's scrap yard there are some brass 4 inch shell cases from the the Great War. My cousin works up at Portland in the stone quarry. They use black powder for blasting and for a bottle of Pusser's rum he'll get me a bag. Drill a hole in the bottom of shell case take the pellets out of a 12 bore cartridge put that in the hole, fill the case with the gun powder and when the firing pin strikes the cartridge it will fire the powder, see,' he explained.

'It sounds a bit risky to me,' said Snowy ruefully. 'We may get caught or even blown up. Whatever happens my missus will still give me hell again.'

'You worry too much, Snowy. You've got to take risks when there's a war on. He who takes the chances wins the game and we don't want to lose this war and be overrun with Germans and have to eat sour kraut do we?' Said Archie.

'What about shells for the gun, we've got to fire some sort of missile haven't we?' Asked Young Pete Hussey.

'Snowy's got some scrap lead in his yard; we can cast some shells with that using a plaster of Paris mould. Stick an iron bar in the middle before it sets to give it some penetration power, it will be just right to knock out one of them German tanks,' explained Big John.

'That lead came off the Baptist Church when it was bombed last month and they will want it back when the war is over,' stated Snowy.

'There you go again, worry, worry, worry. You'll have it back when we've finished with it,' said Archie.

A week later, the boys got on with the job of making the shells and in a couple of hours six were ready.

'They look really good, just like the real thing,' exclaimed Jimmy.

'Do you think six shells is going to stop the whole German army? I only hope that contraption can retreat fast enough,' commented Snowy, shaking his head.

'You worry to much, Snowy,' Denzil said. 'If all else fails we'll block the tunnel at the top of Beaminster Hill with it, that will stop the Nazi's for a couple of hours.'

'Next thing to do is to try out our secret weapon, get her stoked up and on the road,' said Archie, eager to go.

The mighty wagon duly left Snowy's yard, puffing and churning along the road to the seafront. Even Big John had a hard job to steer the big beast, heaving on the big steering wheel. They finally arrived at the front. 'Right, let's try out the gun, then,' said Jimmy. Very keen to see if all the hard work had been worthwhile

After much struggling with the steering wheel, Big John managed to turn the massive machine around to point the gun along the front.

'See that disused public toilet at the end of the beach? Have a go at that, it's no use now,' suggested Archie.

Denzil loaded one of the shells into the gun, closed the breech, and aimed the weapon.

'Ready, **FIRE**!' They all shouted, and Denzil pulled the firing lanyard.

With a mighty bang and loads of black smoke the gun fired at the target. Hitting the old convenience right in the centre with a cloud of dust and out of the other side and hitting the cliff behind.

'Good shot!' They all called out. 'Right in the centre.'

But they very surprised to see one of the Knight girls come running out of the side door waving a pair of white frilly knickers in her hand screaming her head off and quickly followed by one of the soldiers pulling up his trousers'.

'Blooming heck, did you see that?' Exclaimed Archie.

'Lucky they were lying down, or we may have killed them,' said Snowy.

'Why would they be lying down?' Asked young Pete, innocently.

'Never you mind, Pete. Just hope they don't say anything,' said Snowy.

'No they won't, the squaddie should have been on duty at the end of the pier and that girl, which ever one it was, will get hell from her mother if she finds out,' said Archie.

Just then came a moan from the back of the tank.

'Help, help, I'm crushed,' groaned Denzil.

The gun had been dislodged with the blast and he was now trapped under it.

'Don't worry, I'll soon get you out,' said Big John. Grabbing hold of the gun and with a mighty heave lifted it off the poor gunner. 'There, now you're alright,' he said.

'I'm bleeding to death. I can feel blood running down my leg,' he cried.

'Smells more like rum to me,' stated Archie. 'You've broken your hip flask that's all you've done, and I'd like to know where you got the rum from, I bet it's from my shed you old rogue.'
'Well I need it for this dangerous job,' he shouted.

'Well the whole thing works OK. Let's park it up and go for a pint. But first take out the ammunition and put it in the shed. We don't want any one messing with that during the night, do we?' Stated Archie.

They had just put the shells in the handcart when there was a commotion in the square in front of the pub. Marching across in full military uniform with his swagger stick under his arm was Captain C.O.Jones M.C. Followed by four members of the home guard with rifles and fixed bayonets at the slope with P.C.Mock some way behind, trying not too get to involved with this show of strength.
'I demand to know what you people are doing with that piece of unauthorized military equipment? He shouted.
'We made it to defend West Bay,' stated Archie, rising to his full five foot six inches.

'Well, by the power vested in me by the British army, I'm requisitioning this weapon for the defence of Bridport,' he stated, climbing up into the vehicle.
'You men,' pointing to the home guard. 'If that rabble move or try to interfere with my authority you have my permission to shoot them for disobeying a British officer.'
Which was a bit of a laugh, as every one knew that they had no ammunition. But even so the bayonets looked very sharp and the men holding them determined.

Jones pushed one of the levers and the vehicle lurched backwards knocking his peaked cap over his eyes. Adjusting his headgear he pushed the lever forwards. The tank then started to move forward at an increasing fast pace across the square heading straight for the 'George Hotel' opposite, with the four home guardsmen racing on behind. Putting all his weight to the wheel he managed to steer the machine to the left.
'Help,' he shouted. 'How do you stop this damn thing?'
But the boys were too far away to be of any help. Like a runaway train it was heading for the swampy ground by the river, knocking the side off Mrs. Kelly's paper kiosk as it went by. On it went with a full head of full steam, Jones waving his hat and shouting at the top of his voice. 'Help, help, I'm going to die!'
The machine plunged on going deeper and deeper churning it's way into the mud. Even when the water entered the firebox giving off a massive cloud of steam, the

boiler kept it going and driving it on. With a mighty leap the Captain jumped off the back of the vehicle into the muddy water right up to his waist and waded ashore with the help of his gallant men.

The original tank crew had now gathered round and watched in dismay as their majestic weapon disappeared beneath the muddy waters of the river Brit.

'All that time and effort for nothing. That idiot should have gone down with it,' said Maxie.

'I'll have you all thrown into the Tower of London, shot as traitors, hung as criminals, I'll get you for this!' He screamed, shaking his fist and going from red to purple. He was so mad he couldn't say any more. All the lads could do was to burst out laughing at the bedraggled sight, covered in mud and weeds. C.O.Jones turned on his heel and squelched off up the road, followed by his military escort, who were trying not to laugh.

'Well that's that then,' said Archie. 'If the Germans come now we're defenceless.'

'What will we do about the gun? Beaminster will want it back after the war,' stated Snowy, always the worrier.

'If they ask and they're not sure who took it anyway, tell them it was lost due to the incompetence of the army,' said Archie, always the one with a way-out of a difficult situation.

'Let's go for that drink we were about to have, I'm dying for a pint if not two or even more.'

'All that work gone to waste, seems a shame,' moaned Jimmy.

'P.C.Mock kept his head down, today,' said Denzil.

'Yes, he had enough trouble last time with Inspector Hannam,' explained Snowy.

'Ah yes, the Inspector's one of yours as well, isn't he Brother White?' said Archie with a wink.

'Enough of that, I told you before. Must be off now, the wife will be expecting me and I don't want any more trouble in that department,' said Snowy and off they went to the pub, singing. 'The runaway train went over the hill, and she blew, the runaway train went over the hill and she blew, blew, blew, blew, blew.'

Later as they sat in their usual corner in the bar of the 'Bridport Arms' Uncle Lionel said. 'You boys had better be careful, or next time you will be in big trouble. Nearly killing two people, destroying a public building, losing that gun, trying to drown a British Army Officer, knocking a piece off Mrs. Kelly's kiosk and worst of all nearly demolishing the 'George Hotel' opposite and him being a mate of mine. The Germans couldn't have done much more damage if they had landed.'

A month later as they sat talking in the pub drinking their cider. Snowy said, 'Well something good came of it, they have posted 'Cojones' to Plymouth to be in charge of the prison there.'

'The best place for him. He should be behind bars for all the bother he has caused us,' Denzil said. 'With Mock keeping an eye on me I can't even go poaching now.'

'Well at lest those shells makes a useful door-stops to keep the bar door open in the summer,' said Denzil.

'Hope no one kicks them, they might get a big surprise,' Archie commented.

And so ended another saga in the life of wartime West Bay.

THE WEST BAY TANK.

THE UNEXPLAINED BOMB

With the storm clouds of war gathering over Europe in the summer of 1939, one of the greatest fears was the prospect of aerial bombardment and poison gas attacks. This brought home to the public of the United Kingdom the possibility of mass destruction from the air by enemy aircraft flying from bases many miles away.

During the Battle of Britain in the summer of 1940 the German aircraft losses were so great that the invasion of the U.K. was postponed or cancelled. This was followed by what everyone feared, the mass bombing of British towns and cities by the German Luftwaffe. Night after night thousands of bombs destroyed large parts of the United Kingdom.

Consequently one of the biggest operations of the War was the evacuation of one and half million children and their families from the cities of Great Britain to safer areas:

Two families in particular were Davis' and Harris', living in London. David Davis or Dai as he was called, worked for the London under-ground railway and his wife Gwynne worked in the local clothing factory making army uniforms; sometimes the girls there would sew cheeky notes into the seams for the soldiers to read.

They had two sons, Thomas or Tom aged 14, he went to the local Grammar School and Tony aged 12 and a young daughter Megan who was only 3 years old. Mrs Davis' mother looked after Megan while Gwynne was at work. In 1939 the two boys, the young girl and their mother were evacuated to a large farm near the coast in Dorset, Gwen's mother went to North Wales to stay with her relations.

The Harris' had lived in London for many generations, first in the East End mainly working on the docks, but now this particular family lived in Muswell Hill North London. Jack had a very good job as supervisor for the Standard Telephone Company. Mrs Harris, Eve was a teacher at the local infant school. Henry (called Harry) who was nearly 15 went to the local Grammar School with Tom Davis. They also had James or 'Jamie' aged 12 and baby Joy. They had an older boy, Billy, but he was away in the Royal Air Force and was a rear-gunner on Wellington Bombers.

Both families were evacuated to Fair Oak Farm on the coast of Dorset. Their husbands Jack Harris and Dai Davis had to stay in the Capital, as their work was essential for the war effort and the running of the City.

The farm was owned and ran by Walter (Wally) White and his wife Ada. Wally was about 45 years old, a stocky west countryman with a full head of greying hair and always wore a brown trilby hat. Ada a typical farmer's wife, was very homely, her brown hair with grey streaks tied back in a bun, always wore a floral pinny and a shawl over her shoulders and was very involved with the W.I. and the local church. Two farmhands, Ted Childs, over 60 and Fred Bates nearly 80 lived in the village half a mile away and helped on the farm as much as they could. Mr and Mrs White had two sons, Bob and Norman. They had volunteered for the Army in 1939 and were in the Dorset light infantry, later going to France with the British Expeditionary Force to fight the enemy.

It was a large farm on the Dorset coast near Burton Bradstock. Only the wild and windy sand dunes and stunted thorn bushes leaning away from the wind looking like witches hair in the wind, was between it and the English Channel. The farm had many rooms and outbuildings and was quite capable of accommodating the two new families. It was a typical farm of the area, a small herd of cows, pigs, two goats, lots of chickens running around loose and an old horse called Hercules. But it was mainly arable, growing potatoes; wheat or barley and cabbages also hay to feed the cattle in the winter.

When the two families arrived at the farm after a long train journey from London to Bridport then a local bus ride, it had been a long day. Mrs White welcomed them and the first thing she said to young Megan was to ask her if she wanted to sit on the donkey. Megan, wide eyed said 'yes please.' The kindly lady took the little girl around to the back of the farmhouse to a small hut that had a bench with a hole in and said to the child, 'Go on dear have a wee-wee.' To which Megan burst into tears and called for her Mother. 'Mammy where's the donkey?' Megan hadn't realised that this was the only toilet on the remote farm.

They were made welcome and comfortable in this large farmhouse accommodation but were taken aback when they found out there was no electricity or running water. All the water came from a hand pump outside the backdoor. Lighting was by paraffin lamps and candles. Cooking was done and hot water provided by a large coal burning range or stove in the kitchen.

There was also a big open log fire in the main living room to heat the whole house to some degree but in those days most bedrooms were cold and the beds were covered with blankets and eiderdown covers. In winter, very often in the mornings, ice would be on the inside of the windows. Stone hot water bottles or bricks that had been placed in the oven earlier then wrapped in an old towel were placed in the beds to warm them and pushed to the bottom of the bed to warm the feet. A large pot with a handle on the side (called a Jerry) was under each bed for night use and then emptied in the morning in the earth privy outside. A nail was in the wooden side of the toilet and from it hung squares of torn up newspaper threaded on a piece of string; toilet paper was in very short supply during the war. One of the annoying things was to read something new in the paper and not being able to find the rest of the article but it was very satisfying when one found a picture of Hitler or some other Nazi thug. Things were very different in those days and not only on the farms.

The families soon settled in and got used to the animals and the strange smells of the farm. The two small boys went to the village school and the older ones cycled to the Secondary Modern school in the nearest town of Bridport on old bikes the White boys had left behind.

Initially the boys had a bit of bother with the local lads, being from London they were called cockneys or evacs but after a few fights they all became mates and spent many hours playing in the woods or along the river and around the farms.

All the family had to help out on the farm to help pay for their keep and although it was hard work they enjoyed it most of the time, especially the haymaking when Bob and Norman White were home on leave. The older ones were allowed to drink mugs of strong homemade cider called scrumpy and the younger ones larked about in the hayricks; all had a good time.

In 1941 the two older boys Tommy Davis and Harry Harris along with George Eniticott, became apprentices at the aircraft factory in Yeovil, making aircraft parts at the Westland Aircraft Company, staying during the week as lodgers with an old lady (at least 50!) in the town and going to the local Technical College three nights a week to study maths and aerodynamics.

Then going back to the farm and their families at weekends. This suited the boys as they were mad keen on aircraft and spent many an hour talking to the old workmen at the factory about making aircraft, flying and aeroplanes in general.

The old chaps at the factory had many years of experience, some had served in the R.F.C or the R.A.F., also many years making and building aircraft especially the early ones made of wood, wire and canvas and they enjoyed talking to the two young lads. The boys were also very interested in making model aircraft and spent most of their spare time making and flying them.

In early 1942 Sgt. W. (Billy) Harris failed to return from a bombing raid over the Ruhr. The family received a letter from the Commanding Officer of his squadron informing them that he was missing from a raid but believed bailed out and was a prisoner of war in Germany. That weekend all the families were very despondent with the worrying news.

After lunch the youngsters were sent out to play while Mr White had a nap, the mothers gossiped and Mrs White prepared the evening meal. One of the older boys said, as they stood outside in the yard, well wrapped up against the cold Westerly wind. 'I don't know why they have crews in aircraft, they could make pilotless planes, it would save space, guns and all the kit that goes with it and no aircrew to be killed.'
'But it wouldn't be very accurate, with no pilot or bomb aimer,' commented the other.
' Well when Billy was home on leave at Christmas he said that the last raid he was on they missed the target by five miles and that was not unusual,' Harry said, repeating what his older brother had told him.

'I think I could make a small plane based on one of our models, send it over the English Channel with no pilot and a bomb on board and crash it onto the Germans,' said Harry, the oldest of the gang and full of the confidence of youth.
'I bet you can't!' Challenged Tony.
'I bet he could,' shouted Jamie defending his older brother.
'He could, he could.' Megan screamed, for Harry was her hero who could do anything, she then ran back to the farmhouse crying all the way across the yard.
All went quiet after that and they went off to play their different games. Megan came out of the door, with a rag doll in an old pram, singing a nursery rhyme as she pushed her dolly across the yard from the farm followed by Joy now three years old, toddling along with a teddy in her arms and joining in the singing. The two older boys started kicking a football about in the paddock trying to miss the cowpats, the younger ones played with the mud in the small stream that ran near by.

That evening Ada White was in the kitchen baking cakes and pies, the delicious smell cooking wafting through the farm, she later brought in some small fairy cakes for the boys. The two other ladies had gone to the local pub for a drink and a singsong, much to the disgust of Mrs White.

Mr White listened to the latest news of the war on an old wireless set (now called a radio,) that was powered by accumulators that had been charged with electricity at the local garage.

He also liked to listen to Lord Haw-Haw, a British traitor named William Joyce, broadcasting Nazi propaganda from Germany, his opening phrase was. 'This is Germany calling, this is Germany calling.'

Many people listened to him during the war, as he seemed to know more of what was going on than was in the newspapers.

Sometimes there was news of British prisoners, but he wasn't always right especially when he claimed that the German navy had sunk 'HMS Heron' a land based navy station in Somerset. Megan and Joy had gone to bed and the young boys were playing with their model aeroplanes, while the older lads sat at the table with a large sheet of paper in front of them.

'If we had a small engine, perhaps from a motor bike, fixed to some long poles and a light weight wing.' Harry was muttering as he drew lots of sketches on the paper and talking in a low voice so as not to be heard, as the project must be kept secret from the grown ups or it would be stopped before it even started. Also some of the materials would have to be obtained from around the farm without anyone knowing.

'What are you two boys up to?' Asked Ada, coming from the kitchen now she had finished cooking.

'Nothing Mrs White!' Exclaimed the boys, looking guilty.

'Leave them to it,' muttered Wally. 'At least they're quiet and I can listen to the news. Now you two younger ones off to bed!'

'Oh, do we have to?' They moaned.

'Yes, it's 9 o'clock and I want you in church tomorrow morning,' said Mrs White.

Which brought another 'Oh,' from the two boys.

The next morning Tom and Harry, who were excused church now being *workers,* made their way to the local scrap yard on the edge of the village. It was full of all sorts of wonders for young boys. They spoke to Mr Farr, the owner, saying they were looking for spare parts for their bikes.

'OK.' He said. 'But don't make a mess or hurt yourselves.' They looked around for a while and found some old pram wheels.

'Ideal for the undercarriage!' Harry exclaimed. Half an hour later they found the

treasure they had been looking for.
'An engine!' Shouted Tom.
'Shush, Mr Farr will hear you,' warned Harry.

It was a small two-cylinder JAP engine from a three-wheel car that had been in a smash. J.A Prestwich engineering of Tottenham London made the engine for the small three-wheel car built by the Morgan Car Company. It was air cooled and very light. Although it had been damaged, the exhaust smashed and the carburettor broken, the boys were confident they could repair it. Loading all their trophies onto a handcart, they made their way to the entrance when Mr Farr come out of his office and said.

'What have you boys got there then?'
'Just a few bits Mr Farr,' Tom explained.
'Looks a lot to me,' he said. 'I reckon that lots worth about fifteen shillings.'
'Give you ten bob,' Tom was quick to say.
'Dun.' Said dealer, holding out his work worn hand.
Before he could change his mind, Tom put four half-crowns in his palm, saying.
'Thank you very much Mr Farr,' and off they went, pushing the barrow up the lane and back to the farm and into one the out buildings not used by the farm were they planned to build their aircraft.

The days that followed were spent talking to the old workers at the factory, people in the drawing office, teachers at college and working on their plans with the aid of setsquares, rulers, compasses and a slide rule. They found a small old propeller at the back of a shed at the factory, which they smuggled back to the farm.
'Absolutely perfect for the job,' said Tom.
Later they assembled their project in the old outhouse. The engine was stripped down and cleaned. It was ground down or filed wherever possible to make it lighter, the exhaust cut back to just stubs and pieces not required, like the generator were removed. It had a small magneto to provide the spark for its short journey to destruction so no battery was required.

The carburettor was repaired using insulating tape and some thin wire; it wasn't expected to last very long anyway. The engine was reassembled the propeller joined to the crankshaft and the unit fixed to the front of a wooden frame, then four pieces of wood from the frame going rearwards joining at the end for the tail section. They made the tail plane from very stiff cardboard glued to pieces of thin wood.

The wings were made from two planks of wood eight foot long, six inches wide and one inch thick. They drilled large holes along the length to make it lighter and it was tapered towards the tips. Fixed to this were thin laths of wood leading to the trailing edge that was formed with long pieces of wood two inches by one inch. They made the leading edge with cardboard curved over the front and fixed to the main beam with glue and large headed tacks. The whole structure was covered with some old sheets they found in one of the sheds, cut to size and glued to the frame.

The fabric was then painted with a mixture white paint and paraffin, when it dried the material stretched really tight.

Megan left the boys alone with their dirty old engine, which suited them for she'd only tell on them to the grown ups and the game would be over. She would sooner play with Joy and her dolls and teddies and having tea parties on the lawn under an old curtain held up with sticks.

The wings were to be bolted to the bottom of the wooden frame rising at the tips to form shallow V. Thin struts of aluminium would be screwed to the top of the frame then to the middle of the wings to stabilise them. 'Why are the wings like that, Harry?' Asked Tony.

'That's called dihedral to give the aeroplane lateral stability so that it will fly straight and level,' was the informed reply, from someone who had studied at a Tec' college and was now an expert in aerodynamics.

'Oh,' said Tony, not daring to query such superior knowledge.

Next was the petrol tank. To be made from two biscuit tins cut to shape and soldered.

'It will need a slope on it, so that the plane is slightly tail heavy to start with then it will climb to its operational height and as the fuel is used the centre of gravity will move forward and it will then level out for the rest of its journey and when the petrol runs out it will crash onto the target.' Tom explained to his band of wide-eyed warriors.

They had been siphoning petrol from Mr. White's Standard 8 car over a period of time and saving it in a drum at the back of the outhouse hidden behind some sheets of galvanise. The boys thought they were in trouble, when one day Mr White said. 'I don't know why the car's using so much petrol? I only go to market once a week and I seemed to get through a lot of petrol coupons. I hope you boys haven't been mucking about in it.'

'No, Mr White not us. It's because of the war. A man at the factory said that the Government makes it thinner now because there's a war on.'

'Perhaps you're right. Maybe I'll only go into town once a fortnight in future.'

'A good idea,' said Mrs White. 'Then you wouldn't come home drunk so often.'

'That's not fair, I only meet a few old friends, have a couple of ciders and chat about the war, farming and things in general,' he replied.

'Humph! Just a couple, humph, you lot gossip more than a crowd of fishwives on West Bay quay. I don't know what you all talk about for so long? And by the way, where's those old sheets that was in the shed, I can't find them anywhere and I wanted to cover the furniture with them so that I can whitewash the ceiling. It gets very brown now with them two women smoking all the time and your smelly pipe going. I don't know where they get all the fags they smoke? I bet it's from them soldiers and as for you and that pipe.'

She was on a roll now and the nagging could go on for quite a while. But the boys saved the day.

'The goats ate most of the sheets Mrs White, so we threw the rest away,' lied Tommy.

'Them goats are more trouble than their worth, next time you go to market take them with you, I shall be glad to see the back of them.' Then she stormed out of the room.

'I think I'll go for a walk,' said Wally. But everyone knew he was going across the fields to the village pub for a bit of peace and quiet.

The aeroplane was coming on well and was certainly looking good.

'The Wright brothers would be proud of us.'

'The next problem we have is to get the power right; it will need full power on takeoff and reduced revs for the rest of the fight,' said Harry.

Tony who was always full of bright ideas, suggested,

'If we had a long piece of string or twine about a hundred yards long, wind it around a stick, fix one end to the throttle control and the other end to the ground it will unwind like a bobbin. The lever fully open on takeoff then when the string runs out it will pull the throttle back to the three quarter stop and the string is bound to break or slip off the control.'

'There's some old fishing line in the boathouse up by the beach, that will be just right,' suggested Jimmy.

'We'll fix this end to the undercarriage, as we intend to leave that behind when the plane leaves the ground because it wont be landing again,' said Tom.

'How are you going to do that?' Asked Jamie, who always wanted to know the ins and outs of everything.

'We'll fix eight pram wheels to a frame, place the plane on top and as it takes off it will leave the undercarriage behind,' explained Tom.

'What will we use for a bomb, Harry?' Queried Tony.

'We'll use one of them landmines from up on the dunes. Put it in the middle of the plane then it'll go off when it hits the ground and do a lot of damage to somebody,' answered the young man.

'But that's dangerous Harry, it might go off before were we're ready and we'll all be blown to smithereens, what will mum say then?' Said Jamie, looking worried.

'No, they're antitank mines and need a large weight or a big bang on them to make it explode. The soldiers said you can walk on them and they wont go off,' said Harry.

The boys were often up at the camp talking to soldiers and scrounging sweets or chocolate. All sweets were on ration during the war, and the amount per person was only four ounces (about 125 grams) per week. Confectionary didn't finally come off ration till 1951.

Some times they came home with a tin of treacle or golden syrup, which pleased Mrs White, she then made treacle pudding for everyone, lovely especially with fresh cream straight from the farm.

Much of the time the boys had to help out on the farm, hay making, harvesting, lifting potatoes out of the ground and other jobs around the farm to help with the war effort now that most of the men were away in the forces. The root crop in the autumn was hardest work and bitterly cold with the West wind blowing off the English Channel. They complained a lot about this but it did no good and if they moaned too much they got a clip around the head and sent to bed early with no tea.

But they still had time for their project, which was coming on fine and ready to go.

'We should give it a name, what will we call it?' Asked Tom.

'What about the Avenger, that sounds good,' suggested Tony.

'The Avenger, yea great, we'll call this weapon of destruction The Avenger,' announced Harry.

'What's the target Harry, is it Berlin?' Said Tony, the quiet one, but a thinker.

'No that's to far, I think Cherbourg will be a good target,' he replied. 'It's a big port in France, used by the Germans, if we hit that it'll do some damage to the Third Reich and serve then right.'

'Where are we going to launch the Avenger, Harry?' Asked Jamie.

'Down the road to the beach, it's not used now and the army have repaired it so there's no potholes, it will be ideal. We will have to move the barbed wire gate, let the beast go from the top of the hill down the road and she'll go like hell all the way to Europe,' said Tom.

'When are we going to do it, Harry?' Enquired Tony, now anxious to get going.

'I reckon next weekend will be ideal if the weather is right,' he said.

'We need a good wind in the right direction,' explained Tom.

'We've got enough petrol saved, today we'll hide it in some bushes up on the dunes, find a mine and hide that too.'

A week to go and much to be done. They took the petrol up to the dunes and hid it in some gorse bushes, then looked for a mine.

'Careful, find one by the side of the road that's been uncovered from the sand by the wind.'

Jamie shouts, 'I've found one just here.'

'Don't go near it, leave it for us.'

The two big boys carefully lifted it up and started to carry it away when Tom tripped on a gorse root that was sticking out of the ground and the mine fell from their grasp.

'Oh my God!' Yelled Harry, trying to run for cover, Tom just froze and went white; the two smaller boys were running like mad up the road. But luckily the dangerous device landed on some bushes and no damage was done.

'I thought we'd had it' said Tony quivering.

He and Jimmy had returned but kept their distance and looked very scared.

'No, I told you it would take more than that,' replied Harry impatiently now full of bravado but inside he was still shaking. Gingerly lifting up the mine the two boys carefully carried it to where they had hidden the petrol.

'That will do the trick when it hits the Nazis,' commented Harry, giving the explosive device a pat but not to hard as he was still shaken. They then placed more gorse bushes on top so that it was well covered.

The intrepid party returned to the outbuilding and made some final adjustments to the aircraft. All the grown ups had gone to the village taking Megan and Joy with them so the boys gave the engine a test run. After a rough start it went well but they soon shut it down before any one came back and caught them.

'All set now for next Sunday,' said Harry. 'It's back to work tomorrow.'

'I can't wait till next weekend, it'll be fun, won't it Tony?' Cried Jamie, jumping up and down with excitement.

'Shush, be quiet, we don't want the grown ups getting wind of the project or they'll stop It stone dead and all our trouble will be for nothing, plus we'll all get a good hiding.'

It seemed a long week and when the big boys came home on Friday night from Yeovil there was much excitement with the merry gang. Saturday was spent finalising the aircraft and then Sunday morning would be the grand experiment. The big day arrived. The mothers were having a lie in, they had been to the army camp dance the night before, Mrs White had gone to the church early to do the flowers and set out the hymn books etc. and the two young girls went along to help. Mr White was in the cowshed milking his herd and generally pottering about with all the jobs that needed doing on a big farm.

'Right, Tony and Jamie, you push the wings up to the launching site on the handcart, me and Tom will bring the fuselage up on its undercarriage.' Said Harry, who being the oldest had taken charge. 'Don't make a noise, we don't want to get caught at this late stage of the game, do we?'

They made their way to the top of the dunes where they had stashed the mine and the petrol a week before.

'OK, first we have to bolt the wings on to the airframe then screw on the struts to hold the wings firm.'

This job was completed in good time. It looked great with the white wings shinning brilliant in the morning sun, the clean bright engine and propeller in the front of the plane, the long tail going from behind the frame and the whole structure resting on its eight wheeled undercarriage.

'The Avenger looks fantastic,' said Tom, 'just like a real aeroplane.'

'Right, you two, run down and move the gate, while we get the bomb and the fuel.'

Off went the smaller lads to do their duty while Tom and Harry retrieved the mine.

'Careful now, we don't wont a repeat of the last time.'

Gently lifting and carrying the mine to the aircraft they placed it behind the engine and tied it in place with some rope to make it secure.

'That will do the trick when it hits the Germans. Now for the fuel, I've worked out that it will need about three and half gallons to get to its destination so get the petrol and we'll measure it into the tank. I also reckon that with the wind in this direction it'll head straight for the target.' Harry said, holding a compass in his hand and checking the direction. He was now feeling very confident for the success of the project; it was all set to go.

'Right, you two boys hold the tail, Tom you work the controls and hang onto the plane;

I'll swing the prop. Right! Fuel on, switches on, contact, go!'

Harry had done this several times at the aerodrome with a de Havilland Tigermoth.It was quite hard but he gave the prop a good swing. Nothing happened, then again, nothing.

'It's not going, Harry,' said Jamie.

'I know!' Exploded, the bigger boy. 'Give it time.' He was sweating and cursing under his breath using some of the words he'd learned form the men at the factory. He then checked the controls, took out the spark plugs, gave then a good clean and put them back into the engine.

'It looks OK to me,' he said, 'I'll give it another couple of goes. It went all right when we tested it yesterday.'

'Right, here we go again. Fuel on, switches on, contact - Go!' Giving the propeller another mighty swing.

'BANG! BANG! BANG!' The engine roared into life, the whole machine shaking and vibrating, clouds of oily black smoke billowing back across the aircraft making the boys behind cough and splutter.

'We can't hold it Harry!' Shouted Tony, from the back of the plane.

'Quick, Tom, cut the throttle!' Screamed the older boy, frightened that the plane would run him down. Tom pulled the lever back so that the engine just ticked over nicely.

'That's good, now let's get set for takeoff,' said Harry. 'You two boys at the back, hold the tail straight and run as fast as you can, Tom, you hold the end of one wing and I'll hold the other. Fix the line to the throttle control open it wide and let's go for it.'

With the engine going full out and the whole structure shaking, the machine started to move forward down the slope. Soon picking up speed, the boys ran as fast as they could.

The smaller ones soon dropped back but the bigger lads ran quite a way before they fell over into the sand at the side of the road. Quickly getting to their feet they watched their project career down the road towards the sea.

'She's not flying, Harry,' stated the disappointed Jamie.

'Just wait a bit, she'll go in a minute,' said Harry, still full of confidence.

It was just about to reach the end of the road when the plane gently lifted into the air leaving its undercarriage behind stuck in the sand and began to fly on its journey of destruction.

'Hooray, hooray!' Shouted the boys, jumping up and down. 'There goes the Avenger.' Soon the twine went taught and broke, the engine cut back to it's cruising speed and the aircraft carried on with the mission, flying straight, but slowly climbing and then disappearing out of sight into the hazy blue sky.

The boys now stood in silence, quietly gazing at the empty horizon.

'It's gone Harry, hope it gets there and does some damage to the Germans.'

Jamie said, nearly crying.

'She flew like a bird, her's beautiful, the Avenger is bound to get there,' said Tommy, now as proud as a new father.

Just then a loud voice came from behind them.

'What are you boys doing here?' Some one shouted.

They nearly jumped out of their skins and quickly turning round and saw an army sergeant and two soldiers coming across the dunes towards them.

'You boys shouldn't be up here, it's dangerous and didn't you see the notices?' Asked the NCO.

'We've lost our cart down the road,' said Tony pointing at the upended vehicle at the   end of the road.

'Right, you two squaddies get that contraption and bring it back here.'

'If I see you boys up here again you'll be in real big trouble.'

'Sorry mister,' said Tony.

'Mister? Mister?' Bellowed the sergeant. 'You see these stripes?' Pointing to his arm.   'Do you know what they mean?'

'You're a sergeant,' stated Tommy.

'Yes,' said the NCO. 'And don't you forget it,' he shouted.

'I can't wait to get you boys in the army, I'll make you jump.'

'We're going in the RAF,' said Harry.

'Not that pansy brylcream lot?' He exploded, with a look of disgust. 'You want to join a real mans unit like the paras.' Pointing to the winged badge at the top of his sleeve.

'By the way did you see an aeroplane come over here just now and hear three loud explosions?'

'Yes, it was a German twin engine Heinkel, He.111 very low and going really fast. It dropped three bombs into the sea,' explained Harry quickly, before the other boys could say anything.

'I thought it was,' said the sergeant, looking knowledgeable. 'Anyway get off home now before I take my belt to your backside and take that box on wheels with you, it's very dangerous up here.'

The boys scuttled of back to the farm, Jamie and Tony riding on the undercarriage with Harry pushing, and Tom bringing up the rear with the handcart. Everybody was shouting and laughing. They put the two carts in the outhouse and went into the kitchen, still laughing and giggling.

'Where've you been? I've been shouting for you to come in for your dinner for ages' said Mrs White.

'Been up the road with our cart,' explained Tommy, still smiling.

'They've been flying that plane,' said Megan with a crafty grin, 'I've seen it in the outhouse.'

'Shut up Megan,' Tommy said with a look fit to kill. 'It's none of your business anyway.' Lifting his hand to hit his sister.

'Mammy, he going to hit me,' she screamed.

'Enough of that, wash your hands and faces and put some of that Lifebuoy soap round your neck and then get your meal,' shouted Gwynne their mother. 'You're always fighting and arguing, it gets on my nerves, as if I haven't enough to worry about, what with your father away in London and all the bombing.'

'I hate the smell of carbolic soap,' said Megan, screwing up her nose and sniffing as she washed her face. But they were soon tucking into rabbit stew and hunks of bread, all very hungry after the fresh air and all the excitement and exertions of the morning. They then went out to play around the farm and talk about the grand adventure, still very excited.

Latter they went in for tea. Homemade cake, bread and jam and a mug of weak tea but with no sugar as it was on ration and it was needed for the jam and cakes.

'Mr White,' said Harry. 'I'm learning all about engines at the Tec' college, I could give your car a good service, clean the plugs and carburettor, oil the linkage etc. It'll get better miles per gallon after that.'

He was concerned now they weren't pinching the petrol the fuel consumption would improve and Wally might get suspicious.

'No it's alright you might mess it up completely then were shall I be?'

'Harry's very good,' said Tom, 'all the men at the factory say he's brilliant with engines and they let him fix their cars.'

'OK then, but if you ruin it you have to pay to get it fixed at a proper garage like Mr White's.'

'Now be quiet all of you I want to listen to the wireless.'

They all went silent as every one wanted to hear the latest from that traitor in Berlin.

'This is Germany calling, this is Germany calling. This is Lord Haw-Haw to give you the truth about the war. The Russians are being defeated on all fronts and your army in the North African desert is being pushed back towards Cairo and the Suez Canal.' His nasal upper-class voice droned on. 'Today the Royal Air Force lost another bomber, shot down over Cherbourg and all the crew killed in another useless attempt to defeat the glorious Third Reich. When will you British people realise that it is of no avail to keep fighting for your bloated and corrupt leaders against the victorious German army?'

'Turn that rubbish off Wally and put some music on, I'm fed up with that man.'
'All right, dear,' he said. But the boys had heard enough.
'Great,' they muttered smiling amongst themselves. 'Let's go out to play for a bit.'
'Don't be long, you've got work tomorrow,' one of the mothers warned them.
Once in the yard they were full of it, laughing and chattering. 'I bet it was our plane. We did it, we did it,' they shouted.

The next day at the factory Tom and Harry borrowed the *Daily Herald* from one of the men and scoured the paper for news.
'Look, Tom. It says the Air Ministry have denied that any raid took place over France yesterday, in spite of what the Germans have said. It must have been our plane.'
When they got back to the farm at the weekend they told the other boys about the news of the raid in the daily paper.
'It must have been our Avenger that hit Cherbourg I wonder what damage it did?' Queried Tony.
'Shall we do it again, Harry?' Said Tom. Now full of excitement
'No it's too much trouble to get all the bits and pieces and we're bound to get caught if we try it again. It was pretty close last time; I think Mr White was suspicious and as for Megan, well? Anyway I'm going in the RAF soon, I'm just waiting for my call up papers and you'll be joining soon, Tom,' explained Harry.

All was quiet on the farm and life continued with its usual slow pace. The seasons coming and going. Tommy and Harry joined the Air Force and much to their disappointment didn't get to fly but became engine mechanics, serving with Bomber Command at several R.A.F. stations in Lincolnshire; Scampton, Binbrook and Waddington.

I hope you have enjoyed this tale of wartime evacuees in rural Dorset.

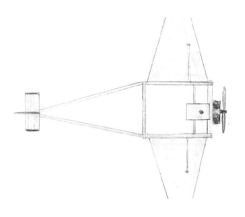

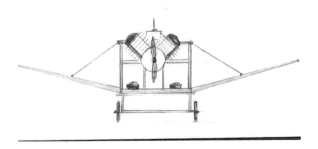

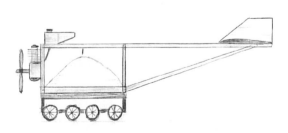

The Avenger

THE NEW BOYS.

The gang was sat at their usual table in the corner of the 'Bridport Arms' on a Sunday evening in 1944. They had just finished a friendly game of skittles, and were tucking in to a plate of cheeses sandwiches, pickled onions and pints of cider.

'Well you young lads, off to join the forces tomorrow then? Said Snowy, to Pete and Jimmy.

'Yes, we had our medical at Exeter. Never been that far before,' said Jimmy. 'Went to Dorchester once but didn't like it. The Germans have really knocked Exeter about. The whole of the centre of the city has been wiped out.'

'But you didn't get in to aircrew did you Jimmy?' Asked Denzil.

'No, they said I had flat feet, but I can't see what difference that makes,' replied Young Westcott.

'If you got flat feet you can't bail out because you'd land too heavy and break your legs, and then you couldn't escape,' explained the knowledgeable Archie

'Anyway I've volunteered for the Navy now, Motor Torpedo Boats. That should be fun and I think I've got *some* experience in that field!' He stated. 'So I'm going to H.M.S. St. George in Portsmouth tomorrow.'

Pete said. 'I'm off to West Kirby tomorrow for basic training, I've no idea where it is but I've got my train ticket and instructions. I take the train from West Bay to Dorchester change trains for Bristol then Crewe and find a train for this place called West Kirby.'

'That's near Liverpool, went there once when I was in the Navy.' Said Archie, 'horrible place it was.'

'My Mum wouldn't let me fly, said it was too dangerous and I might hurt myself,' moaned Pete. 'So I'm going into the electrical and wireless branch, it will be useful when I come out.'

'What are you lot going to do without us two doing all the running about for you when we've gone?' Asked Jimmy.

'Well, there's those two Brown boys, Curly and Ginger. They're always hanging about the quay looking for something to do,' said Maxie. 'They left school at Christmas when they're were fourteen and can't go into the Navy till they are fifteen.'

'They'll be good lads, quite big and strong, and they like a drop of cider too,' said Denzil. 'They'll be ideal and they have a younger brother Steven but they call him Shorty, he'll be useful running errands, and we can keep then out of trouble.'

'Not much hope of that,' said Snowy, shaking his head.

The Brown boys live in North Street in Bridport with their mother who worked at Chant's bakery. Mr. Brown was away in the Navy and had been gone most of the war. He was on H.M.S. Exeter when the British Navy fought the German pocket battle ship, the *Graf Spee,* which was scuttled in the entrance of the River Plate in Uruguay on Hitler's orders. They were good lads but a bit of a handful for their mother, always getting into some scrape or other.

The new lads soon settled in with the routine, which meant doing as little as possible. In-between ducking and weaving, a bit of fishing and trying to make a few bob on the side. But it didn't take long before P.C. Mock was around, saying that the boys had been see scrumping apples up on the Squire's estate.

'I'll have a word with them,' said Archie. 'They'll be no more trouble, you see.'

A few days latter, when they were out fishing Big John threw the boys over-board. Then hauled them in by the scruff of the neck.

'That will teach you not to give us any more trouble. Next time we'll leave you to swim back.'

'Yes, John,' they both said. Now soaked to the skin and very subdued. They never caused any more bother and were very willing helpers until they went into the navy.

Shorty, Curly and Ginger with Tacker Robins.

THE AMERICANS

'Over paid, over sexed, and over here.'

The arrival of one and half million American service men, at the end of 1943 to June 1944 for the invasion of Europe caused quite a stir in the United Kingdom. No more so than in Dorset. Thousands were stationed in and around the county. Camped in fields, billeted in houses and anywhere that was available. They were friendly young men away from home and were made very welcome. Children shouted. 'Give us some gum chum,' and they gave them gum, sweets, etc. American comics like Captain Marvel were highly collectable by the local boys. The only downside was that the local girls found them more attractive than the British men. With their smart uniforms, plenty of money and that American accent. The other disturbing factor was they drank every pub dry in the district. Even so they were welcomed into homes, gave parties for the children, and spare food to the population.

'Seems a shame we can't get in on the act,' said Archie, as he sat drinking with his mates, in the corner of the 'Bridport Arms' one Sunday night.
'Yes, them Yanks with all that money, it don't seem right do it?' Denzil moaned.
'Issy Isaccs is doing well selling them cider. The cinemas are packed, and the fish and chip shop in Bridport sells out every night,' Curly Brown said.
'That's it!' Exclaimed Archie. 'We catch loads of fish, cod, haddock, whiting; we can get plenty of potatoes from White's farm at Burton Bradstock. We could set up a mobile fish and chip shop by their camp.'
'My brother Tom, he has a butchers shop and a slaughterhouse up at Broad Windsor. He can get lots of beef dripping and pigs lard, just right for frying,' said Big John.
'What are you going to fry them on?' Asked Ginger Brown.
'A couple of big pans my missus uses for jam and fruit,' explained Archie. 'Put each one on a brazier like the workmen use.'
'I'm good at filleting fish, been doing it all my life,' said Denzil.
'Who's going to peel the spuds?' Asked Curly.
'Why are you all looking at me and Ginger for?' He said in fright.
'Well someone's got to do it and you two have just volunteered, or I'll give you a thick ear,' threatened Big John.

A week later the gang were outside the American camp. With Snowy's truck decked out with a big tarpaulin stretched over the back, they were in business. The young boys were peeling the potatoes, Denzil preparing the fish, Big John cooking the chips and frying the fish and Archie serving and taking the money.

'Come and get your fish and chips here. Half a crown a time,' he shouted as he wrapped them up in newspaper, adding salt and vinegar if required. Soon they had a queue and were doing a very brisk trade. When Snowy had queried the price with him, Archie just said. 'Well now see. Two and two is five, half of five bob is two and six which is half a crown, 'in it? It's easy, you just went to the wrong school that's all,' he explained.

Then came two White Caps, or Military Police. 'And what in the darn hell is going on here?' One of the policemen asked.

'Well it's like this Officer, we are just doing a service for our American cousins,' Archie explained, always polite to anyone in authority.

'Now take these, they are on the house as you Americans are such good people,' thrusting a portion into each of their hands.

'Gee thanks,' they stuttered, taken by surprise.

'Anyway, the Camp Commander has just sent his batman over for some, so it must be alright,' he said.

'Well OK then, but don't cause any trouble,' warned one of the M.P.s.

'No sir, we know how to behave, we're British, and I was in the Royal Navy in the Great War,' said Archie, giving them a smart naval salute. And off went the patrol eating their food.

So ended the first of many good days.

'That was a great,' said Maxie. As they were counting the money in the corner of the bar, making sure no one else could see.

'About twelve pounds ten bob, and a couple of American coins,' announced Snowy.

'Time we paid for the fish, potatoes and fat, give Snowy five bob for petrol and the use of his lorry, it's about two quid each and ten shillings for the young lads,' said fly Archie.

'Hang on,' said Snowy. 'Eight pounds plus two ten bobs and five bob is nine pound five shillings.'

'Well I got make a profit, haven't I, and I caught the fish and bought the potatoes,' explained Archie.

There was a bit of rumpus from the rest of the gang, but he quickly said. 'Alright then I'll get the drinks in and we'll leave it at that.' Going up to the bar and ordering ciders all round. Which then seemed to satisfied the rest of the boys.

The trade went on for quite a few weeks and they were doing very well, no one seemed to trouble them. The G.I.s were glad of the service and the change of diet from their usual food. As they were paid monthly and as they like to gamble, some of them ran out of money towards the end of the month, so they received things like tins of chopped pork called Spam, tins of meat and veg, K rations, sweets and chocolate in lieu of money. Even Snowy managed to scrounge a couple of gallons of petrol for his lorry.

'I'm fed up with spam,' complained Archie one day. 'My missus gave me fried spam for breakfast, spam fritters for tea and I even had spam sandwiches when I went out fishing yesterday. And she reckons we're having spam salad for tomorrows lunch.' 'Well it's better than tin pilchards,' said Curly.

They didn't go every day so not to push their luck, but twice a week. Usually Monday and Thursday.

But as always. All good things must come to an end at some time. On Monday the 4th of June 1944, they packed the truck with all their gear and set off up the track to the camp. Parking the lorry and looking around, Maxie said. 'It's very quiet in' it?'

'They've all gone, the whole place is empty,' exclaimed Curly.

'It's deserted, there's no one here at all,' cried Young Ginger.

Indeed much to the surprise of every one in the district, the troops had moved out over night to Weymouth for D-Day and the invasion of Europe. A couple of locals were looking around for souvenirs or anything that had been left behind.

'They gone to invade France,' one explained.

'Well I'm blowed, no one told us about this, it don't seem fair after all we've done for then,' said Snowy. 'Leaving without a word

'Well, that's it then, back to fishing and farting once more I suppose,' said Denzil.

'But it was good while it lasted,' said Archie, philosophically

Six American Gi's Just before D-Day 1944

From the left. Evo Valenti 23, from New England. Killed in France August 1944. Neil Gebhart 19, wounded at Aachen, the first town to be captured in Germany in November 1944. Edwin Guillerstrom 19, from St. Louis. Killed in Normandy 1944. Sylvan Chargo, 19, from St. Paul, Minneapolis. Killed in Normandy 1944. Frank Ganas, 40, also from St. Paul. Captured in Normandy. Louis Fabrini, 19. Captured in Normandy 1944

In the first day of D-Day 6th June 1944 a thousand Americans were killed on Omaha Beach.

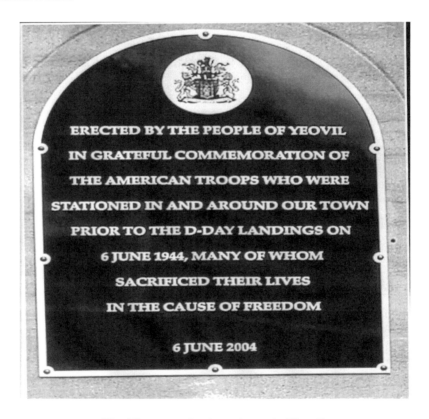

The Plaque to the Americans in Yeovil.

THE WRECK

The motley gang sat in their usual corner of the 'Bridport Arms' with empty glasses in front of them. All the lads were looking very down in the dumps. Even the two Brown boys weren't their usual jolly selves. 'Uncle' Lionel didn't mind them being in the bar as long as they behave themselves and with the War on thing were more tolerant.

'I've never been so poor in all my life,' said Archie. 'Fishing's bad, they reckon all the bombs, depth charges, activity and fuel spilt in the sea during the invasion of France has driven all the fish away or killed them off.'

'I might have to get a proper job if things don't buck up soon,' moaned Maxie.

A week later in their same spot, things seemed a bit brighter.

'Had a good catch today,' announced Archie. 'So the drinks are on me.'

'Blimey, it must have been good!' exclaimed Denzil.

'Also,' went on Archie. 'My cousin up on Portland said that during the D-Day invasion a U.S. transport ship carrying twenty Jeeps and fifty Harley Davidson motor bikes lost it's power got into the Portland Race and was swamped by the sea and sunk.'

'Well what are we going to do about that then? If I think what I'm thinking, no I'm not getting involved with you lot again,' said Snowy, shaking his head.

'It's easy, we find the wreck, drag up a few bits as salvage and Bob's your Uncle. I've got a brother-in-law in Bristol, I know he's a bit of a Spiv but he'll get rid of the gear for us and it will be a few quid in it for us,' explained Archie.

'I think it's illegal, you can't just go around dragging up Government goods and get away with it,' said Snowy.

'How can it be illegal, it's just like fishing. You puts down a hook and what comes up is yours, whether it's fish or a bit of scrap metal,' explained Archie. 'They don't complain when we pull up a mine and get rid of it for them for nothing do they?'

'How are we going to find the ship, attach a hook and bring up the goods?' Asked Big John.

'Well, in the harbour master's store is an old diving suit, we'll borrow that for a week or two,' said Archie, who always seemed to know the answers to everything. 'It might need a few patches but Snowy can do that with his Vulcanising machine.'

'And who's' the one to go down?' Asked Big John.

'Well you are qualified or so you said once,' said Maxie.
'But that was years ago in the last War,' he shouted.'
'It's like ridding a bike, you never forgets,' said Denzil.
'Then you better go down, anyway the diving suit's to small for me,' stated Big John.

A week later, just off the Portland Race was the *Mary Lou*. Denzil dressed in the diving kit, the two Brown boys pumping the air pump; the intrepid explorer was lowered over the side and into the dark waters off Portland Bill. Making sure no one from the shore could see what they were up to. They soon brought up some of the ex military equipment.

It wasn't lifted on board till were on the way back out of sight of land. Then it was hauled aboard and covered with tarpaulin and brought ashore when it got dark. Although the gang considered what they were doing was OK there was no reason to let the whole world know what was happening.
On one of the trips there were six sharp tugs on the line from below. This being the emergency signal they quickly pulled up the diver.
'Blooming hell,' exclaimed Denzil, when they opened the front of the helmet.
'I've just seen an eight foot conger eel, with a head as big as a Jack Russell dog, and teeth to match. Gave I a hell of a fright, could have bitten my arm off.'
'You should have stamped on it with those big lead boots, they fetch good money at the market,' said Maxie.
'Bugger off, I an't going down there again today.'
'Here have a slug of rum, you'll be alright,' said Maxie, handing him a bottle of Pussers.

The Jeeps and motorbikes were in good condition as they were covered in a heavy layer of grease and hadn't been in the water that long. They raised 15 US Jeeps and 30 Harley Davidson motorbikes during the next couple of weeks and most of the ship had been cleared, when a storm blew up and shifted the wreck into deeper waters beyond their reach.
'Well we did well out of that, got a few quid in the old tin box,' said Archie.
'What do you reckon we made, Archie?' Asked Denzil.
'Well, my Brother-in-law, Charlie, gave me 200 quid for each Jeep and 50 for each bike,' said Archie.
'That's four and a half thousand pounds,' exclaimed Snowy, quick as a flash. He hadn't gone to a Grammar School for nothing. 'And I bet you had a cut as well.'
'Only a small fee for all the work I did. If it wasn't for me we wouldn't have

anything and it was my boat. I thought we give the boys ten pounds each, giving us just over eight hundred each.'

'More profit, Archie?' said Denzil.

'Of course, It's only natural in' it,' Archie said, with a broad grin.

'I might get another boat to replace the old *Lorna Doone,*' said Big John.

'I might take on a pub,' said Denzil.

'My Vera wants a bungalow in Weymouth,' said Archie.

'I wouldn't mind taking on Mrs. Korputs' paper kiosk, I thing she wants to sell it soon. It would be a nice little earner,' said Maxie.

Snowy said. 'I might retire, I'm getting too old for all this excitement.' For although he tried not to get involved, he still joined in the enterprise.

Just then into the pub came James, the Squire's butler.

'Ah, Mr. Brookes, a note from Sir John if you don't mind. He said to give it to you personally. It seems rather urgent. Must be off.' With that he left the bar, climbed onto his pushbike and cycled off up the road.

'Blimmy,' said Maxie. 'What was that all about?'

'You'd better open it quick and see what it says,' said Denzil.

Archie opened the letter with trepidation and read the contents.

'Well what does it say? Ask Snowy. 'You've gone very pale, must be something up.'

'It says I've to go up to the Hall as soon as possible, an matter of urgency,' he explained.

This put a bit of a damper on the rest of the evening and they soon went home.

The next morning Archie was up at the Hall before nine o'clock to find out what the problem was. Mabel greeted her friend at the kitchen door. 'Hello Archie, the Squire will see you straightaway. I'll call James to take you to see him,' she said, with less of her smile than usual.

'Mr. Brooks Sir,' James announced, as he showed Archie into his master's study.

Sir John was looking out of the window, overlooking the large estate. Much of the grounds had been ploughed up for potatoes, barley and other crops to help the War effort. As he turned round to greet his guest he looked very serious and didn't invite him to sit-down this time.

'I have quite a major problem on my hands.' He hesitated and eventually said.

'Brooks. The Chief Constable of Bristol, who is a personal friend of mine, went to Eton together. He telephoned me yesterday. It appears a lot of United States military equipment has cropped up in his area and has asked me if I can throw any light on the subject. I have made a few enquiries and it may have come from a wreck off Portland Bill, which I am told by the authorities has now been washed into deeper waters beyond recovery. As the Americans are our greatest Allies it is very embarrassing and I said I would look into the situation and let him know. I have come to a very hard decision. As you well know Lady Dorothy is very involved with charities, her favourite being the local church. She tells me it needs a new roof. Dry rot, deathwatch beetle, woodworm and some of the lead has disappeared and my good Lady would dearly wish to help in this worthy cause. The cost would be about four and a half thousand pounds.' He let the words sink in for a minute, then said. 'I think if a large donation was left at the church, I could inform the head of the Bristol Police, that having looked into the matter no one in this area appears to be responsible, and I'm sure the matter will be dropped. Perhaps you could look into it, Archie?'

'Well I'll see what I can do, sir,' he said quickly.

'Yes, I'm sure I can rely on you to do something about it.'

With that the Squire summoned his butler and Archie hurried on his way.

'Blooming heck, what are we going to do? I'm too old to go to prison,' moaned Snowy when they met later in pub, and Archie explained the situation to his mates.

'We will just have to do as the Squire suggests, there's no other way out,' said Big John.

'Seems a hell of a shame, after all the hard work we done. But it is going to a good cause,' said Denzil.

A Huntley & Palmer's biscuit tin stuffed with white fivers was duly left at the high Altar of the local church and a discreet word whispered into James the butler's ear. The matter was closed.

'Lucky I got a spare motorbike over. I didn't tell 'e we pulled up 31, did I? So we got fifty quid still. Eight pound each of us and ten bob for the boys,' explained Archie.

'You old rogue, Archie,' said Maxie. 'You always were a crafty blighter.'

'Any way, five eights is forty, two ten bobs for the boys, that's forty-one pound. Where's the rest?' Asked Snowy.

'Well I got to make a profit, haven't I?' Explained Archie.

'We had better get back to some fishing, or we'll not have any beer money tonight,' said Big John.

And so ended another event in Wartime West Bay.

1944 U.S.Jeep.

THE SMUGGLERS

'Things be a bit quiet around here, nothing going on at all. I'm fed up with just fishing, no excitement these days,' said Archie.

'What do 'e expect, all the action is in Europe,' explained Maxie.

The lads were sat in their corner of the "Bridport Arms."

'All that money being made on the black market in France, cigarettes, coffee and nylons stockings going for fantastic prices. It makes me sick,' moaned Big John, taking a great gulp of his cider.

'I don't see why we can't get in on the act?' Denzil commented.

'Where are we going to get the goods from?' Asked Maxie.

'Well, I've got an idea,' said Archie.

'Oh no, not again,' cried Snowy, remembering the last time.

'Well I'll explain. Then you can all see if it's OK. I've got a mate down in Fowey. Now he's got an old Baltic trader named the Bolgen, built in 1919. It's been stuck up the creek in the mud of the river Fowey since the war broke out. He brought some timber over from Sweden in 1939 and couldn't go back because of the war. The bottom's a bit rusty and the engine needs a bit of looking at. He said we could have it for free as long as we take it away because the authorities want it moved or they will charge him rent and he's off to join the army soon. I'm sure we can fix it. A friend of mine is doing some building repairs for the council in Plymouth and he will give us some concrete to seal the bottom, use some chicken wire to reinforce it. Maxie can fix the engine then we can bring it back here,' explained Archie.

'What then?' Asked Snowy, fearful of the reply.

'We go across to America and get some ciggies, coffee and nylons of course,' said the exasperated Archie.

'But that's smuggling!' Shouted Snowy. 'We'll all end up in jail, and what with Captain Jones in charge we'll be in real trouble.'

'Shush, we don't want ever body to hear. Anyway you worry too much, Snowy, you always did. I had a great uncle in the Napoleonic days he used to bring stuff over from France all the time, swapping English cloth for French brandy with those dammed Frenchies in the eighteen hundreds. Then one day the Northover boys shot him. They ran all the illegal trade from Lyme to Weymouth in those days. They say they shot a revenue man once up Osmington Mills way but it was never proved.' Said Archie.

'That would have been Benbow Northover, the one they called the Pimpernel. A right rogue he was until one day his luck ran out. He was eventually hung by the neck till dead in Dorchester prison. Or 'stabbed with a Bridport Dagger' as they say. Because in the old days Bridport use to supply the hemp rope to the Tower of London, as well as the most of the rope to Royal Navy.' Explained Big John.

'He weren't the Scarlet Pimpernel, was he?' Asked Ginger.

'No,' went on Archie. 'That was years before, during the French Revolution. This one was called 'The Black Pimpernel' because he was a bit on the dark side. They say one of his ancestors was foreign like; story goes she was an African Queen captured by Sir Walter Raleigh in 1580 and brought back to Plymouth, where she married a local lad and the family latter move up to Dorset and married into the Northovers. Another of the Northover boys, young Robin, a right young tearaway from Sturminster Newton was also hung for sheep stealing at about the same time. All the trouble caused their poor mother to go to an early grave. He only got caught because his young cousin Jack Penny, who was on lookout, had too much cider and fell asleep in the ditch. Young Jack was sent to Portland prison but escaped and joined the Navy, no questions asked in those days. He then deserted his ship in Boston harbour in America, married a rich widow and was eventually murdered by her eldest son, or so the story goes anyway. And so will we be hung if we are caught, that's if we live that long,' Snowy continued.

'Cross the Atlantic in an old leaky boat with a concrete bottom and a duff engine, you must be crazy. I thought last time you wuz mad, this is just plain stupid,' exclaimed Snowy.

'How are we going to buy all this stuff in America, we a'nt got any money?' Asked Denzil.

'Well it's like this,' explained Archie. 'With all the bombing there's loads of old furniture about; even the Squire has a barn full of the stuff. We can get it for nought just to take it away. Them Americans will pay good money for our antiques.'

'Antiques? It's a load of old rubbish,' said Snowy.

'But they don't know that do they. Anything over fifty years is antique to them. We just write 'Queen Anne or George 111' on the back of some, drill a few holes to look like woodworm and they will fall over themselves to buy it. By the way how do you spell Chippendale?' Asked Archie.

'How do I know? But I'll give the trip a go. I'm fed up here doing nothing and I need the money,' said Denzil.

'So will I. I've nothing better to do,' said Big John.

And so in the next couple of weeks, the old M.S. Bolgen was restored to some sort of resemblance to a sea going vessel and duly sailed to West Bay harbour, to be loaded with antique English furniture. The concrete bottom was given a coat of tar and seemed fairly watertight. The twelve-cylinder diesel Volvo engine was taken apart by Maxie and given a good overhaul. It misfired occasionally but sounded quite good. Archie managed to scrounge some diesel fuel from Portland in exchange for some lobsters and they were all set to go.

'Look out, P.C. Mock is on the war path,' said one of the boys.
'What's going on here then?' He asked.
'We're just taking this old furniture to Ireland for the poor people there as part of a humanitarian act on our part. We hear they are a bit desperate over there owing to the wartime blockade. And do a bit of fishing on the way back,' explained Archie, always one with a quick answer.
'Well make sure you don't go outside national waters, there is still a war on I'll have you know, not that it makes any difference to you lot.'
'That's not fair, Constable, we do our bit for the country,' replied Archie.
'And for yourselves,' said P.C. Mock, as he walked away.
'Right, let's get going before he come back with some sort of warrant. All the gear stowed, rations on board, plenty of water and fuel?' Asked Archie. 'It could be a long trip this. You young boys had better stay ashore, I don't want any trouble from your mother.'
'Oh, can't we come? It'll be exciting,' moaned the young boys.
'No, and that's final,' said Maxie.
'I'm not going either,' stated Snowy. 'My wife will give me hell again.'
'Oh yes you are, we need you to read the charts and speak to the Americas. You sound better than us, with your public school accent and you can give them the proper handshake,' stated Archie, the Commander of this new expedition.
'Well OK then, but don't tell the wife. I'll just say I've go the go to London on very important business for the Squire and can't divulge it because it's secret,' he said reluctantly.
'I told my missus I 'ad to go to France to help with the invasion,' said Maxie.
'I said nothing to mine, she will just think I'm on the p--- again with you lot,' Big John said.

The next morning, just as dawn was breaking the M.S. Bolgen left West Bay harbour on its export mission. The old Volvo engine was coughing, spluttering and belching out a cloud of black smoke. The bilge pump was doing well, pumping out a stream of oily water over the side, even the seagulls kept their distance.
'Oh my God,' cried Snowy, being sick over the side for the second time. 'I'm going the die and I haven't been to confession lately either.'
'Oh shut up you old Jonah, I put two shillings in the poor box in St. John's

church by the harbour this morning, that should look after us for a while. Anyway get breakfast going I'm hungry,' said Denzil.

The old Baltic trader made a fair speed; they kept well away from the shore so as not to attract any attention from the authorities. Crossing Lyme bay, passing Torquay and Start Point heading west. The sea was quite bumpy, the currents and wind were against them, but they made Falmouth late afternoon and anchored for the evening. They didn't fancy sailing by night at this stage of the journey. They tied up the ocean going vessel along side the quay in Falmouth docks and went ashore as sailors do.

In the dockside pub that night they met many old sea salts that knew Archie and his escapades very well, especially the Roscoff episode. The drink flowed well, trying to judge the different qualities of Cornish and Devon cider. Then Archie brought a bottle of Pusser's rum from his jacket pocket and the party really got going. At about midnight it was finally decided that both ciders were as good as each other and all went back to their respective beds very happy.

The next morning the motley crew were a bit late rising.
'I feel a bit fragile today,' said Big John. 'I recon that cheese we had was a bit off last night. What do you think Denzil?'
'Yes I'm a bit hazy myself, must have been the cheese or them pickled onions. Shan't have them again,' he replied.
Slowly they got their proud vessel started up and on the way to America.
'Westward Ho!' Shouted the intrepid adventurers as they sailed out of Falmouth harbour heading west towards the new world and new opportunities.
'Let's have some breakfast, I'm starving,' said Big John, rubbing his large stomach. 'I feel ill,' moaned Snowy.
'Yeah, let's have some bacon and eggs,' said the Brown boys, who had just appeared from the lifeboat.
'How the hell did you get onboard?' Asked Denzil.
'We weren't going to miss a trip of a life time, were we?' Was the response.
'I'll tan your ass before long, now get the breakfast going and earn your keep,' shouted Big John.

During the day the sea became a bit lumpier, the diesel engine had begun missing on two cylinders, shaking the boat and the bilge pump was working overtime.
'We seem to be taking in more water than we are pumping out!' Stated Snowy, always the worrier.

'I think the concrete is cracking; it's that dam engine shaking the boat to bits, there's a lot of water coming inboard, we may have to stop soon,' said Denzil.
'Stop! Where? We are in the middle of the blooming ocean. This is worse the being up the creek without a paddle!' Exclaimed Snowy, beginning to panic.
'We will have to pull into the Isles of Scilly for some repairs,' stated Archie.
'More like the silly islands for me,' said Snowy.

Three hours latter they were heading for one of the southern islands, St. Agnes.
'There nowhere to land, we will just have to head for a beach,' said Archie.
'There is no beach just rocks,' said Big John.
'There's a cove dead ahead, go in there,' shouted Denzil.

The Bolgen hit the pebble cove with a shuddering grind and came to a halt. Their proud boat began listing to one side and the sea came crashing over the stern. The crew scrambled ashore and turning round saw their lovely ship being pounded by the surf and the wooden cargo floating in with the tide.

'Well, that's that then,' said Maxie. 'All our efforts gone for nothing.'
'Not quite, we were insured for two hundred pounds. That's fifty quid each, as it cost us nothing,' said Archie.
'What about us?' Asked the boys.
'You'll get nothing; you're a pain in the bum. If you're not careful I'll give you both a thick ear and I'll tell your mum,' said Big John.
'No, don't tell our mum, please,' they pleaded.

The next day our heroes managed to salvage quite a lot of the cargo and sold it to the locals for a few quid to pay for their fare home. They say there are still a few antiques on the islands fetching good money. Some claiming they are from Sir Cloudsley Shovell's ship, the H.M.S. Association that sunk with the loss of all 800 hands when it struck the Gilstone Rock along with three other Royal Naval ships.

The shipwreck crew managed to get a boat ride to Penzance with someone Archie knew and then a train to Bridport. Much to their delight no one seemed to have missed them and no questions were asked. But P.C. Mock did give them a strange look next time he saw them. He just shook his head as he walked by and said nothing.

The next day Uncle Lionel was pleased to see them back in their usual corner of the pub, spending their ill-gotten gains. But Aunt Liza gave them a very black look; those dark eyes sent shivers up and down their spines.

'She may be good looking but she gives I the creeps,' said Big John, taking a mighty gulp of his cider.

'She could give me a couple of creeps any time, I'd take a chance on dying just for the pleasure.' said Archie, with a wicked grin.

'You'll end up in Hell you will,' stated Snowy.

'Yeah, but what a way to go,' was the reply.

And so the smuggling episode passed into local legend and life carried on in West Bay as usual.

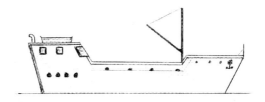

M.S. Bolgen

THE PRISONERS OF WAR

As the local lads sat in their usual corner of the Bridport Arms, Denzil suggested. 'We ought to go fishing tomorrow, or we will run out of money   and what will we do for cider and beer then let alone food?'

'There is fog coming in from the west tomorrow morning, it don't look too good,' stated Archie, the more experience of the gang, and skipper of the Mary Lou.

'We should still go anyway, we needs the money, I'm stony-broke. We will just have to use the compass,' explained Big John.

'I don't like the idea of that, we will be in trouble again,' Snowy said, shaking his head, always the worrier.

'Don't worry, Snowy, Archie will get us 'ome OK, 'e always does,' said Denzil. 'Get some beer in and see if 'Uncle Lionel' can put it on the slate?'

Early the next morning the Mary Lou set off from West Bay harbour into the swirling mist to the English Channel fishing grounds. It become very foggy during the day but they still sailed on for several hours only catching few fish.

'We might as well get the frying pan out and have some thing to eat,' suggested Maxie.

Soon the hungry crew were tucking into fried Spam, eggs and fried bread, with lots of tomato ketchup, washed down with mugs of tea laced with rum.

'Have you got much more of this American tomato sauce left, Archie?' Denzil asked.

'About twenty 1 gallon jars, plus three hundred tins of Spam, enough to see the war out I recon,' replied the Skipper.

'There don't seem to be many fish about today, we've been sailing all day and only caught about twenty Mackerel so far and a couple of codlings, they must be all sleeping,' said Big John.

'Ah, they don't like this weather, nor do I,' said Archie. 'And I don't like the look of the sea either, there be some thing wrong with it, it don't look right.'

'What's wrong with it?' Asked Snowy quickly.

'It's the wrong colour for where I think we should be. Let me check the compass and have a look at the chart again. There's some thing wrong here. Who put this dammed iron horseshoe up on the shelf? It's made the blooming compass wrong all day, no wonder we're not where we should be.'

'Well I put it there; my Mum gave it to me for good luck. I didn't know it would make any difference to the compass,' explained Curly Brown, looking very shame faced. 'I'm sorry,' he muttered, apologetically.

'You ought to have known better. It's made of iron and that will always affect a compass, every body knows that. Can tell you weren't in the Sea Cadets or the Boy Scouts. Any way what's done is done. Now we'll have to find our way 'ome,' said Archie, looking around for inspiration.

'Now we're in trouble again, I knew it would happen. I never learn do I?' Moaned Snowy. 'If you was clever you would be dangerous,' he said, looking at the boy. Archie was about to through the horseshoe over the side of the boat, when Snowy screams. 'Don't do that, or we'll have more bad luck. All I want to do is go home.' Just then Maxie shouted. 'The fog's thinning, I can see land over there, look!' Pointing to port.

'Yeh, but where in Hell are we? It could be any where on the Planet for all we know,' stated Snowy, now looking really worried.

'Well I don't recognize it,' said Denzil.

'There's a small harbour over there to the left, looks bit like Polperro or Mevagissey,' said Big John.

'Well I'm not too sure. It don't look like anywhere I've ever been to before. We'll come along side the jetty tie up and find out from the locals. If we can find any, it don't look like there's anyone about,' said Archie.

'Well I'm taking my shot-gun, I don't trust them Cornish, they used to be wreckers in the old days, killing any one that was washed ashore,' said Big John.

They tied their fishing boat along side the granite quay and jumped ashore.

'There's some soldiers over there, let's go and ask them where we are,' said Denzil. The motley crew walked towards six soldiers idly standing in a group under the shelter of the sea wall. Big John was leading the way with his shogun under his arm.

'Just a minute, they don't look like Tommies to me?' Queried Maxie, who had been in the British army. 'Blooming heck, they're German, I can tell by their helmets,' he shouted. Big John pointed his gun at the group ready for action.

With that the soldiers spun round. Seeing the crew of the *Mary Lou* approaching, dropped their rifles threw their hands in the air and shouted, 'Kamarad!'

'Blooming heck, they're surrendering, what shall we do?' Said Snowy.

One of the Germans said in broken English. 'For us ze vor is over, Tommy, ve are your prisoners. Ve are too old to fight.'

'Where are we, what is this port?' Asked Archie, keen to know where he was.

'This is Braye harbour in Alderney, in the Channel Islands. The var in Europe has passed us by. We vant to go to England,' said the soldier.

'Hell, we're miles off track, quick let's get back to the ship and go home,' said Snowy, keen to get away.

'What about these Germans?' Asked Denzil.

'Well we can't leave them here or they will raise the alarm. Get them onboard the boat quick before any more turn up and want to go to Blighty,' said Archie.

The soldiers were soon bundled aboard; the crew jumped in with their captured weapons. They quickly untied the vessel, cast off, started the engine and were on their way home as fast as their old fishing boat would go.

'I bet the Northover boys from Dorset were here in the old days, carrying out their smuggling activities. Swapping English cloth for French brandy with them dammed Frenchies during the Napoleonic wars of the eighteen hundreds,' said Maxie.

'That would have been Benbow Northover, a right rogue he was. The one they called *The Pimpernel*, till his luck ran out and he was eventually hung in Portland prison. Another one of the Northover boys, young Robin, a right terror from Sturminster Newton was also hung for sheep stealing at Dorchester prison about the same time. Their poor mother went to an early grave,' explained Snowy. 'And so will we if we're not careful. What a booming game this is,' he said. 'This will take some explaining when we get back, that's if we ever get home again. We will be in real trouble, and my missus will give me hell once more.'

'Don't you worry so much Snowy; it'll be OK. Let's get some food going, I'm starving,' said Archie.
Soon they were all tucking into thick hot bacon sandwiches with mugs of cocoa with a good dash of navy rum. The Germans were diving in with gusto.
'Ve have not had such good food for a very long time, there is very little on ze Islands, only fish, rabbits and sea birds. The German authorities has abandon us, and the allies don't vant to know,' said one of the old German soldiers, who spoke a bit of English.
Maxie, who had been in the army in the First World War, and learnt a few foreign words when he was in France. He often called his wife. 'Me petty waso,' (my little bird,) was soon chatting away to them in a mixture of English, French and German, like old friends.
'Well, would you believe it? It looks like me and him were on the Somme together in 1917. Different sides mind you, but we all suffered the same. It was the lads on the front line, German and British that had all the hardship. Mud deep enough to drown a horse, while the big wigs sat in their chateaus well behind the front lines drinking wine and cognac and tucking in to fra-grass. It wasn't our war anyway; I never understood it, just because some Austrian Archduke got shot. And what with our King George, the Kaiser and the Tsar of Russia being cousins like. Some blooming family dispute that was, millions were killed. Anyway this bloke here is called Heinz; he seems a nice sort of fellow, got a family in Dortmund, or what's left of them. Mum and Dad killed in an air-raid, a brother on the Eastern Front and hasn't heard from his wife or kids for ages.'
'Well I don't like all this collaboration with the enemy, don't forget they bombed our chip shop in Bridport,' said Denzil.
'I think we should shoot them and put the bodies over the side. I saw this film once; "No prisoners taken,"' said young Ginger Brown, who had only know war in his short life. 'Our dad's away in the Navy, he was injured on H.M.S.Exeter at the battle of the River Plate with the German pocket battle ship, the Graf Spee. Our house has been bombed and we got to live with me Auntie Doris, a right old battle-axe. Now we're chatting away and feeding them. It don't seem right some how.'
The German soldiers, all were aged over fifty, caught the gist of the conversation and went quiet.

'Ve vont no trouble, ve hate Hitler and ze Nazis, all ve vont is peace,' said Heinz, putting his hands on his head. So all went quiet and they sailed on into the night, most of them getting their heads down, apart from Archie steering the ship, Snowy still worrying and Big John keeping guard on the prisoners.

The next morning they sailed into West Bay harbour, tied up along side the quay and unloaded their meagre catch. They were just bringing their prisoners ashore, when along comes P.C. Mock on his bike.

'Well, what have we here then?' He asked.

'Well, it's like this constable. We were out fishing and we just happened to catch these German soldiers,' explained Archie, never one to go into to much detail. He always said. "The more you say the more trouble you're be in."

The Policeman, who had heard most things in his life before was dumfounded.

'I, ah, well, um. There's no room at the Police Station for them it's only got one cell, I'd better phone the army,' and he quickly rode off on his bike

'Blimey, that was a change. What shall we do with them? Said Denzil.

'Best knock on 'Uncle Lionel's door and take them into the pub. If we explain he will understand, may even get an early pint,' said Archie.

'Well, I'm off home, I don't want any more to do with this,' said Snowy and with that he shot off home.

'Uncle' wasn't please to see them at that time of day, but once Archie had explained the situation to him he let them all into the pub. But 'Auntie Hilda' made sure they didn't get a drink, not even a cut of tea. Her jet black Dorset Six Toed cat (a polydactyl), called Merlin, raised the fur on its back, hissed at them then scooted off up onto the top shelf at the back of the bar, and gave them an evil look with its one eye.

'That cat's evil,' said Denzil.

'You leave my cat alone, or you'll have me to deal with,' 'Aunt Hilda' said, giving them a black look, and then she turned around and stormed off into the kitchen.

'We better get outside before she comes back,' said Big John. Ushering their prisoners out and carrying the captured weapons out onto the forecourt of the pub. Less than half an hour a jeep pulled up outside of the pub followed by a five-ton army truck with six squaddies aboard. From the jeep jumped a short army officer, peaked cap, Sam brown belt, with a swagger stick under his arm. He quickly marched up to the group, gave a smart salute

'Colonel Adrian Prentigast-Smith. M.C. Somerset Light Infantry. Well you chaps. What is going on here?' He demanded, looking at the motley crowd now gathered outside.

'Well, it's like this sir. We was out fishing, the fog came down, our compass went wrong and we ended up in Alderney and these Germans surrendered to us, so we had to bring them home, see?' Explained Archie.

'You've no right swanning about capturing Germans. That is the job of the army. I've a good mind to make you take them back!' He shouted. 'I want a full written report on my desk first thing in the morning.'

'Well now see, sir, that could be difficult. As I can't read nor write. Now when I was with Lord Jellicoe in 19--.'

'That will do, Brooks,' said P.C.Mock, who had just arrived. 'We've heard it all before. I'll do the report, Sir,' giving the Colonel a salute, hoping perhaps for a little kudos, and maybe make sergeant.

'All right, carry on Constable. Right. You men get these prisoners and their weapons aboard the truck and keep them covered with your rifles,' the Officer ordered his troops. 'We don't want them escaping.' He said.

'Well, that was a turn up for the book. I think we got away with that,' said Archie, smiling and giving his mates a wink.

'I haven't finished with you lot yet,' said the Policeman. 'You are still in deep trouble. I'll see you all later,' and off he cycled up the road.

'Pity he don't fall off his bike and break his flipping neck,' said Big John.

'We could get 'Aunt Hilda' to put a curse on him, or set her cat on him. That would fix the old so and so,' suggested Denzil.

'At least we got six German helmets out of it, they must be worth a couple of bob each,' said Archie, always one to make a profit.

'Never even got a cup of tea. I think we deserve a blooming medal,' moaned Maxie.

'We were lucky we weren't shot as spies by either side,' said Snowy who had just returned to find out what was going on.

'Don't worry, Snowy, only the good die young, so that lets us out,' stated Archie, skipper of the *Mary Lou*.

No more was heard about this strange episode from the authorities or the Police Constable, even Snowy's wife was quiet, so perhaps they did get away with it.

THE DAY ARCHIE WAS SHOT

The local fishermen were stood on the quayside at West Bay harbour, looking out to the rolling sea of Lyme Bay.

'I think it's too rough to go out today,' said Archie. 'Especially after the last time we were out. I can't afford to lose my boat, it's all I got'

'I agree. I thought we were all going to die; them Germans could have shot us. What have you got there, Maxie?' asked Snowy.

'It's a mine detector. My cousin was wounded on D.Day and sent home. He brought it with him from Normandy as a souvenir. Now he has given it to me for looking after his missus while he was away.'

'Oh Yeh! You're good at that,' said Denzil.

'And what are you going to do with it? Although I could make a couple of suggestions,' said Big John.

'I just thought when the war is over; I could go on the beach and find some money with it. People are always dropping coins when they are changing into their swimming costumes. It's better than fishing anyway,' said Maxie.

'But you're supposed to hand it in to the authorities, or it's stealing,' said Snowy.

'It's not, it's beach-combing, finders keepers, that's traditional,' explained Archie.

'I thing we should try it out first. The playing fields would be a good place to start. The kids are always rolling around up there and losing their pocket money,' suggested Denzil.

Later, they were hunting all over the recreation ground and finding lots of pennies and halfpennies. Then they found half-a-crown (12 ½ p).

'Blimey, before the war you could buy five woodbines (cigarettes), go the pictures, afterwards buy a pint of cider, a penny bag of chips and have enough left over to get the bus home,' said Denzil.

'Cost more like five bob or even more now,' said Archie. 'Them Yanks have spoilt it for all of us.'

'I think we should try up on the downs, where the army was camped before D.Day. British and the Americans troops were there for a long time. There must be plenty of stuff up there,' suggested Snowy, now getting into the action, and thinking of lots scrap metal to be obtained.

The next day they all piled into Snowy's lorry and headed for the old army camp. Before long Maxie was out in front waving his metal detector in front of him. Every time he heard a buzz one of the boys put a tent peg in the ground, and the rest started digging where the pegs were. Soon they were finding brass cartridge cases, army buttons and cap badges, lots of coins, English and American. They even found some lorry batteries.

'Worth their weight in gold,' said Snowy.

'I've got some thing big here lads, the machine's gone haywire!' Exclaimed Maxie.

'Stand back!' Said Big John. He then took hold of a pickaxe, swung it over his head and into the ground. As it hit the ground there was an almighty bang, blowing the big follow several feet back, singing his hair and eyebrows. He staggered to his feet, his blackened face bleeding from several small cuts.

'Blooming heck, I must have hit some live ammo and it exploded.'

'Well it would do, it don't just go "pop", does it. You was lucky,' said Denzil.

From the back of the crowd came a groan.

'I've been shot bad, I think I've had it this time me old mates,' moaned Archie, lying on the ground groaning with blood coming from a wound on his right arm. 'Look after poor Bess for me when I'm gone,' he whispered to the rest of the lads, as they bent over their wounded comrade.

'Bess?' Queried Curly. 'He hasn't got a dog.'

'No, he means that widow next door to him,' said Snowy. 'Anyway it's not that bad, only a bit of shrapnel in you arm. You'll just have to drink with the other hand.'

Denzil pulled his shirt away to reveal a small piece of metal protruding from the top of his arm. The ex-sailor takes a pair of pliers from his tool bag and was about to pull it out.

'No! It's going to hurt,' screams Archie. With that, Big John hit him under the jaw and knocks him out cold and while he was unconscious Denzil pulled the bit of metal out. 'There, nothing to it,' he said, holding up a small piece of metal. Denzil then poured some rum from his hip flask over the wound and tightly bandaged it with a couple of clean handkerchiefs.

'There, that should be OK now,' he said.

Archie slowly come around, shook his head and asked. 'What happened, I feel like I been hit by a bus.'

'It's OK; you just got a slight scratch from a bit of shrapnel on the arm. Let's get you down to the pub, after a couple of pints you'll feel fine.

Here have a slug of rum to be going on with,' said Denzil.

'My arm is a bit sore, but I don't understand why my jaw hurts so much? I must have hit it on the ground when I fell down.'

'Yeh, that's right, you did fall a bit heavy,' explained Big John, not willing to let on that it was he had hit him.

Back at West Bay the gang piled out of the truck and into the pub. Two of them holding Archie up.

'You look a bit pale Archie,' said 'Uncle Lionel'. 'You OK?'

'He just had a slight accident, that's all. Get him a pint of Guinness with a glass of port in it, because he's lost a bit of blood and needs the nourishment,' explained Denzil.

'I've seen worse than that before now. You should have been on the Western Front in 1916,' said Maxie.

'Auntie Hilda' then came into the bar and gave the casualty a worried look. She took his weather beaten head between her hands, stared into his eyes and muttered some words in Romany to him. Archie eyes glazed over and he seemed to go into a trance. The dark haired beauty stepped back, clicked her fingers, turned around and was gone.

'Blimey, what was that?' Said Archie, shaking his head. 'I feel great now, all the pain's gone.' He then reached for his pint of stout. 'Aah!' He shouted. 'I thing I might sill have to drink with my left hand for a bit, and me shirt's ruined, the one I got off the Americans, it was a good one at that.'

'Well, at least we have some money for a while, it should last till the end of the month when the mackerel season starts,' said Denzil'

'It'll last us the rest of our lives if we ever do that again. We were very lucky again this time. I'm never ever doing that again,' stated Snowy, sinking his pint in a couple of gulps. 'I'll have a double whisky now to calm my nerves.'

'I recon we must have a guardian angel,' said Maxie.

'More like the Devil looks after his own',' stated 'Uncle Lionel'.

THE BAD PENNY

'You looked chuffed to bits, Archie,' said Big John. 'Missus left 'e?'
'No, not that good, Squire just gave I four bottles of port. 'e reckons we did a good job with those Germans. Some thing like humanitarian, what ever that means.'
'It means we were kind to our enemies in defeat,' explained Snowy, the clever one.
It was fairly early on Saturday night in the 'Bridport Arms'. The lads were on their first pint, perhaps one of many. The door opened and in walks a small weather beaten man wearing a smart suit.

'Blimey! It's Jacky Thorn!' exclaims Archie. 'I haven't seen you for ages. I thought you'd gone on years ago.'
'Only the good die young, he's like a bad penny, they always turn up,' said Maxie.
'Let's see now, last time I heard you were sent to Borstal for three years for pinching a boat,' said Snowy.
'He should have been hung. He sank old man Penny's fishing boat and that was his living, he died broken man,' said Archie.
'Oh great, it's nice to see you boys as well. Anyway, let bygones be bygones. Let me buy you all a drink, I've only got gold sovereigns, but I expect 'Uncle Lionel' will take them?' With that he puts a couple of shinny gold coins on the bar.
'Blimey! I 'aint seen one of them for a very long time, well I'm not one to bear a grudge, mine's a pint of the best and a whisky chaser,' said Denzil.
'In that case I'll have a bottle of Guinness and a large glass of port, I still don't feel too good after my accident,' said Archie, rubbing his right shoulder.

Soon they were all drinking to the good health of their long lost friend.
'Well then, what have you been up to since we last saw you?' Enquired Big John.
'It was like this. I couldn't stand that Borstal. It was worse than being at home with my mum. Up every morning at half past five, bullying, and terrible food, six of the best across you arse for nothing, so I did a runner after a couple of weeks. Went to London where I met some young students in a pub from Cambridge University who were off to Spain to join the civil war there. I thought that sounded like a good adventure so I joined them; we got a boat to Bibao in northern Spain and became part of the International Brigade. I didn't know they were all communist did I, a lot of Bolsheviks. Anyway we had a bit of a battle with some Royalist troops and I got shot in the arm, not bad though but enough to be sent to a hospital in Madrid. Then General Franco who was in charge of the Spanish army in Morocco joined in the war. So I thought dam the commies I'll

join him, he seems a better bet with a proper army and regular food not like that toffee nosed Cambridge lot, paella and Spanish brandy and their "Cheers old boy." I still kept my arm in a sling but it didn't do any good. They gave a rifle and there I was in Franco's army. He wins the war and takes over the government. I thought that's it I'll go on somewhere else, but no, I'm in the Spanish army now and sent to Morocco. It was all flies and heat and as for the food, rice, olive oil and garlic with a bit of smelly fish all served with rough Spanish wine that tasted like vinegar, I've put better stuff on my chips. So me and a couple of the other blokes decide to do a bunk over the border to Algeria. But crossing the border we meet a French patrol, with no more ado they starts firing at us. I get a crack on my swede from a bullet and when I wake up with a sore head I had a big bandage on my head like a turban. I'm now in a French prison and my mates have scarpered, then the guards find some funny tobacco made from a local weed in my pack. Their officer says I'm to be shot at dawn the next day for smuggling drugs. I thought my luck was up this time, but he suggested that I could join the French Foreign Legion and no questions asked. Well I've seen the film Beau Guest and thought this sounds romantic, so I said all right. Next thing I'm out in the blooming boiling hot desert middle of nowhere with a lot of foreigners. But at least the food was good with gallons of beer and loads of better wine and once you got use to the life it was OK. The legionaries were a hard lot but good mates when they got use to you and knew you could take care of yourself, with plenty of drinking singing and fighting with the locals in the bars of Algiers. The life was tough but with litres of wine a day and plenty of beer we were never sober enough to complain. Then the Second World War starts and Germany attacks France but the Legion is not allowed to serve in the home country so we are sent to Lebanon, which was then part of the French empire. This was a cushy number with loads of women, good food and wine till the French surrendered in June 1940 and we became part of the Vichy army now on the German side.

The British invade Lebanon and now were fighting the British and me being an Englishman but I now spoke French, Spanish and a bit of German. We had a bitter battle; a Legionnaire has only one country, the Legion. So we did our best but we were out gunned and out numbered. We wuz about to surrender when I whips off my uniform and stick on some civilian cloths I had in my pack. I was about to make a run for it when I gets shot again, this time on the left arm by a British soldier. It wasn't too bad just a flesh wound and I end up in hospital in Cairo. I crack on I wuz a British business-man working in Beirut selling jewellery and just got caught up in the war and lost all my goods and papers. I don't know if they believed me or not, but an officer says. 'Right, you are a British citizen and are now conscripted into the British army.' So I end up in the blooming British Eighth army under Montgomery fighting Rommel in the western desert. There I was minding my own business, crawling along, keeping my head down with my tin hat on and I get shot in the arse by a German. Sent back to Cairo and discharged from the army as unfit for duty but I still had some sovereigns I managed to scrounge doing a few deals with some Arabs in Lebanon.

So here I am,' says Jacky.

'Blooming heck!' Said Big John. 'You've been shot by the Spanish, the French, the British and the Germans and end up here with a load of gold coins. You were very lucky or your telling us a very tall story.'

'You always were a bit of liar Jacky; I mine the time I got the blame for braking Mrs Dalwood's window. You did it and told her it was me then I had to pay for it and got a wallop of my old man when all the time I was swimming off the beach,' moaned Maxie.

'I'll show you my scares if you don't believe me,' he was about to pull his trousers down.

'Enough of that,' shouts Uncle Lionel. 'You'll upset my missus and then there will be trouble for all of you.'

With that, 'Auntie Hilda' comes into the bar and gives the adventurer a look that could kill. Jacky went very pale and said. 'I must go now,' and shot out of the door. As he crossed the step the landlady snapped her fingers and pointed at the fleeing man. He trips and falls flat on his face, rolls over a couple of times, picks himself up and races off up the road.

'Well, what do you think of that!' exclaimed Archie.

'Good riddance is all I can say,' said Maxie.

'Well he left his money on the bar, we may as well have some more drinks,' said Denzil.

And all had a very good time and Jacky Thorn was never seen in West Bay again.

HE ALWAYS WAS UNLUCKY

'Thing are a bit quiet at the moment', said Snowy, as the lads sat in their usual corner of the pub one evening. 'Can't get enough petrol to sell, no new cars, and those that got an old ones don't want to sell them. Just a few repairs and the odd spare part, that's all.'

'Nothing much happening anywhere. The only thing I heard was Jack Dyer's packing in the undertaking business. He's getting too old and his sons are away in the forces and don't want to know. Anyway he said trade's dead,' stated Denzil, with a chuckle.

'There's money in that game if ever there was. Stick them in a hole and charge what you like,' commented Archie.

'Burial at sea is cheaper,' said Big John. 'Did that to my old dad, only cost ten quid.'

'That's it!' Exclaimed Archie. 'Snowy's got that old black Humber car; I've got the boat. Collect the body from the morgue, wrap it in an old bit it of sail cloth, a few chains around the feet, sail out a couple of miles, over the side and Bob's your uncle. Easy money.'

'Must be more to it than that. You can't just go chucking bodies over-board like that,' said Snowy, always the worrier.

'Well I'm going to look into it and let you know,' said Archie, always one to look for some easy money.

'In the old days of sailing ships, they uses to sew the corpse in his old hammock and it was the custom to put the last stitch through the nose to make sure they were dead. Weighted body with a cannon ball and over it went into Davy Jones's locker,' explained Big John.

A week later they were gathered together again.

'I've found out all about it. All you need is a death certificate and a form the Registrar of births, death and marriages to dispose of the body, and permission from the Harbour Master, which is me,' explained Archie. 'Let's put an advert in the local 'Echo' and see what comes up.'

'Drinks are on me, lads' said Archie, a few days later. 'Got a call today from Mrs. Blackthorn. Her husband Alf has been killed down in Plymouth. He was a store man at the barracks there, an unexploded bomb had laid undiscovered from the air raids in '42. They were knocking down some old sheds and it went off and killed him. Alf always was unlucky. Went out with his missus once, before they were married I'll have you know. Never again, she was a real moaner, and you should have known her mother, what a dragon? Anyway she wants us to do the funeral, burial at sea. O.K?'

'But he was never in the Navy, hated the sea, couldn't even swim, he use to live next door to us before the war,' said Snowy.

'Ah but, I said we could do it for twenty quid plus a pound for the wreath. Wants a cheap job, she always was a tight one. My missus will make a wreath for two shillings, her being in the W.I. It will be a few bob in it for all of us, a bit of money for a couple of beers at lest,' explained Archie.

'Well if you say so, Archie. We'll give it a go, but I think we're messing with things we know nothing about, delving into the unknown and the unnatural, I don't like the sound of it at all,' moaned Snowy, shaking his head.

'You'll be alright, I'll look after 'e,' said Archie.

'That's what I'm afraid of, something will go wrong, and it always does.'

Two days latter, when they met. Archie explained to the group.

'I've got all the paper work sorted out. We go to Plymouth tomorrow morning about eight o'clock, collect the body wrap it up in some sail cloth, 'cause he don't look to good, what with the bomb and all. Put him in the back of the truck and take him straight to the boat. Put the corpse onboard on a large plank out stern of the ship, put a few chains around his feet, and cover him up with a big Union Jack. All set to go everybody? Snowy! You fetch Mrs. Blackthorn and her mother in your Humber, also the vicar. He weren't to keen, but I explained he owes us a favor after we paid for the new roof on the church, so he agreed.'

They all came aboard the boat, Mrs. Blackthorn, her mother, Snowy, in his bowler hat, dark suit, black tie, white gloves and a sprig of acacia in his lapel, Archie in his harbour master's uniform, and the vicar was looking very somber. All the crew in their best clothes, even Big John put on a clean shirt. The two Brown boys wore their navy cadets uniform with white lanyards, black ribbons etc, looking very smart.

The funeral barge set off out into the open sea. It wasn't long before the two ladies; the vicar and Snowy were seasick over the side of the boat, for it was a bit of a heavy sea.

'Better go a few miles out,' whispered Archie to Denzil who was steering the funeral vessel. 'We don't want the goods drifting ashore do we? And we don't want other people knowing our business, or we may get stopped or even worse they'll all be at it before long. I think we got to go three miles out anyway.'

After a while Archie said. 'This is far enough. Stop the boat Denzil but leave the engine running.'

The sea had calmed down by now. All the mourners sang. 'Eternal Father---All those in peril on the sea'. The vicar said his piece and at the point when he said. 'We will commit his body to the deep,' the two Brown boys lifted up the end of the plank and Alf's earthly remains slid gently into the water with a small splash. Mrs. Blackthorn flung the wreath onto the sea, saying. 'Seems a bit of a waste, all them nice flowers.' Maxie started to sound the Last Post on his bugle as the boat pulled away.
'Got to do a good job, could be more of these,' said Archie.

When there was an almighty explosion from behind the ship, sending a plume of water forty feet into the air. The body must have hit a sunken mine. Mrs. Blackthorn screamed and fainted, the vicar and Snowy were sick over the side again. Big John shouted. 'Blooming heck!' And the boys reckoned they saw Alf's face in the spray.

The widow's mother shouted at Maxie. 'It's all your fault, we're not paying for this, and it's a right palaver.'

'I didn't do it,' moaned Maxie. 'Don't blame I.'
Denzil headed the boat for the harbour as fast it would go. No one wanted to hang around, what with Snowy and the vicar being sick again, the women wailing, complaining and moaning, the boys were looking deathly white as if they had seen a ghost, and the rest of the crew wanted to get back ashore as soon as possible. Once they were back in harbour, Snowy took the ladies and the vicar home in his car and didn't come back; the Brown boys scarpered off somewhere, still frightened to death and weren't seen for several days. The rest of the team went to the pub.

'Well another fine mess, we might as well have a drink, ' said Maxie.
They entered the pub and regaled 'Uncle' Lionel with the disastrous affair.
'Well at least before you all went off, Mrs. Blackthorn left ten shillings for a bit of food, but that's all. Got a couple of pork pies, some spam sandwiches and a jar of silver skin onions, the ones you only get at funerals,' said 'Uncle'.

'But I'll give you a pint each, I reckon you deserve it after what you did for poor old Alf, he wasn't a bad sort of chap.'

'Blimey, that's a first, you giving us a beer,' said Archie.

'Make the most of it, it could be your last, you're all a lot of no-goods,' said 'Auntie' Hilda. Giving the lads a cold look with those piercing blue eyes. She snapped her fingers and an icy draught went through the pub and the lads shivered and a crack of thunder rolled in from the sea.

'Blooming heck, put on other log on the fire quick, I feel like someone's walked over my grave,' said Big John.

A couple of pints latter they all burst out laughing, as they all said together.

'He always was unlucky.'

And so ended, and perhaps the last episode in war time South Dorset.

THE PEACE AND AFTER

Peace in our time: A celebration paddle at West Bay 1945.

The end of the war in Europe in April 1945 was a bit of an anticlimax. After the initial celebrations thing went back as before, shortages and rationing. The war with Japan still went on until the unconditional surrender on the 15th August 1945.

The West Bay fishermen carried on as usual. Big John bought a second-hand boat with the compensation money he received for the *Lorna Doone* and Denzil joined him as a crewmember. Archie with Maxie's help went on fishing and wheeling and dealing, Snowy pottered around in his garage.

Pete Hussy was not demobbed straight away but was sent the Far East. Serving in India, Burma and then going to Australia, eventually coming hone in 1947 to a very different England. He bought a small shop, selling and repairing radios and was one of the first to be involved with Television.

Jimmy Westcott served on M.T.B. boats in the Mediterranean and stayed for quite a long time after the war, clearing mines etc. When they were demobbed Jimmy went back to fishing with Big John.
The Brown boys stayed in the Navy, married some local Plymouth girls and lived in Devonport by the docks.

The White boys came back to the farm. The two evacuated families left, Billy came home having spent over three years as a prisoner of war in Germany.

Harry and Tommy were demobbed and the families were reunited, but with many happy memories of their life in Dorset and for years the smell of new mown hay always reminded them of those happy days on the White's farm.
The Harris' and the Davis' had to find new homes as their old ones had been destroyed in the bombing of London and went to live in one of the new towns built especially outside the Capital.

The two older boys married a couple of girls they met at the local dance hall and moved to Dagenham to work at the new Ford factory. The younger ones were called up for National Service and joined the Air Force for two years, serving in Suez, Cyprus and Germany.

Beaminster asked for their gun back but was told the Army had destroyed it. The Baptist Church was repaired by the War Damage Commission so did not want their lead back and Archie's brother-in law did six months in prison for black market offences.

After the war enquires were made by the boys and it appears that from the records on that particular Sunday in 1942 a plane of unknown origin had crashed onto a warehouse in the Cherbourg dock area and set fire to paint store causing a large fire and a great deal of damage to the Docks.

Neil Gebhart the GI wounded in Germany, spent some time in the Military hospital in Yeovil, returned to St. Paul in 1945 and was still alive in 2005. A plaque in honour to the Americans stationed in the area in 1944 was put up in Weymouth, Beaminster and Yeovil.

In 1946 William Joyce (Lord Haw-Haw) aged 39, was hanged in Wandsworth Prison on the 3rd of January 1946 as a traitor. Although he was born in Ireland and was an American citizen, he had lived in England, held a British passport and owed allegiance to the King and was therefore guilty of treason. He was the last person to be hung for treason in Britain.

And lastly one of the Knight girls had a baby nine months after the shelling of the old toilet, must have been the shock.

Uncle Lionel's funeral

SOME OF THE LOCAL CHARACTERS.

THE SECRET BOMBER OF WORLD WAR TWO

In 1941 the Battle of the Atlantic was at its height. In Marsh & April of 1941 German U-boats, surface cruisers and pocket battle ships sank over 1.000.000 tons of Allied merchant shipping. From 1939 to 1945 U-Boats sunk 2,200 allied ships, 14 million tons. At a cost of 734 German submarines, 28,000 sub-mariners were killed, four out of every five who went to war in U-boats
The Prime Minister, Winston Churchill stated. "If we lose The Battle of the Atlantic we lose the war."
The Nazi U-boats had the United Kingdom in a stranglehold and the grip was getting tighter. In the autumn of 1941 German submarines sank the battleship H.M.S. Barham and the carrier H.M.S. Ark Royal while acting as convoy escorts in the Mediterranean.

The food ration was reduced in September 1941 for the third time of the war. Also 30% of the shipping losses were oil tankers bringing vital fuel to Great Britain, especially petrol for the Bomber Offensive against Germany, as this was the only weapon we had to strike back at the enemy who now occupied nearly the whole of Europe.

At a Cabinet meeting in October 1941, Lord Beaverbrook, the Minister of Supply and Aircraft Production, stated that the production of four- engine bombers, like the Halifax and Stirling was going well. The new Avro Lancaster four-engine bomber could fly at over 20.000ft and carry 14.000lbs of bombs would be handed over to No.44 Rhodesian Squadron in December. They were delivered on the 24th of December, what a Christmas present! Unfortunately raids on Germany may have to be restricted because of the lack of aviation fuel due to the shipping losses. At the same meeting he said the production of coal was at it's highest since 1913, the year of the biggest output ever in the U.K. Some wag at the back of the room remarked, 'The Great Western Railway Company would soon be making steam-driven aeroplanes to bomb Germany,' which raised quite a laugh and much amusement.

The Prime Minister was only five years older than Beaverbrook a him very well. They had both served in Lloyd George's Government in 1917. Churchill as the Minister of Munitions and Aitken. (Now Lord Beaverbrook) The Minister of Information. When the meeting was closed, Winston called his friend back. 'I say Max, what do you think about this steam powered plane. You remember that chap Stringfellow from Somerset don't you? It is just possible it may be found to work. Look into it and see what you can find out and report back to me.'

Winston Churchill was born in 1874 and would have heard of John Stringfellow, an engineer in the lace industry from Chard in Somerset who died in 1883 when Churchill was nine years old, Churchill and Stringfellow were also Freemasons. Stringfellow had built a steam powered aeroplane in 1848 which flew 20 feet, thought it was unmanned it was the first powered flight of a heavier than air vehicle in the world. The next year in 1849 he built another model with a ten-foot wingspan that flew 120 feet at the Great Exhibition held in 1851 at the Crystal Palace in Hyde Park London. 20 years later in 1869 he built a Tri-plane. This had a steam engine and a boiler weighing less than 13 pounds producing over 1 BHP. Through lack of backing he failed to develop it any further. He became a very prominent Mason and businessman in Somerset and lost all interest in aviation. A replica of one of his aircraft is in the Science Museum at South Kensington in London also the Museum of Transport in Washington D.C. U.S.A. And in Chard Somerset there is a museum to his name.

On the 9th October 1880 a Frenchman Clement Ader piloted a spirit-fired steam engine aircraft 650 feet at Armainvilliers near Paris, 15 years before the Wright brothers short hop, but for some reason it was never recognized.

The Besler was a steam-powered biplane using fuel oil. Piloted by William Besler it flew over Oakland California on 12th April 1933. Nathan Price designed and built the 150 hp two-cylinder reciprocating steam engine. The ideal was not taken up. He later worked for Boeings and then Lockheed's where he helped develop their first jet engine.

Churchill was always interested in any new idea or innovation, especially if it would help the war effort and many weird and strange inventions were tried out during the war.

At the beginning of the war, W.W.1 "ace" Cecil Lewis tried trailing cannon balls on cables from the hatch of a Wellington Bomber in order to intercept incoming enemy bombers (Lewis obituary Daily Telegraph 1997).

During the war Rockets were attached to large wheels to run up the beaches with explosives fixed to the wheels to blow up the enemy defenses. Sir Percy Hobart, a favourite of Winston, was one of the pioneers of tank warfare. He designed the special and unusual tanks for the "D" day landings on Normandy, the Crab, Crocodile, Ramp and Bobbin tanks.

Lord Mountbatten in 1942 when the Allies were planning the "D" day operation, said, "If we can't capture a port we must take one with us." This idea was greeted with much laughter at the time but two years later,

"The Mulberries" were unloading troops, tanks, ammunition, etc. on the beaches of Normandy. Even Barnes Wallace's bouncing bomb was a very strange and unique device and at the time it was thought a crazy scheme and had no chance of success.

Winston was also First Lord of the Admiralty 1911-15 and in 1939. He was secretary of state for war & air 1919-21 and knew that the Royal Navy had steam driven "K" class submarines, he was involved with planning, saying on the 28th October 1914, that "steam engines may be used to supplement oil engines in these boats. The "K" class submarines had two steam driven turbines for surface propulsion, four electric motors for under water and an auxiliary diesel engine. The vessels weighed 1700 tons, were 338 feet long and had a surface speed of over 22 knots. When diving the boilers were put out, the funnels retracted and the boat then ran on battery power. Seventeen were commissioned between 1916 and 1918 and the last one to be scrapped was the M3 in 1932. Without exception they were a total disaster, as Lord Fisher a former First Sea Lord said in 1913. "The most fatal error imaginable would be to put a steam engine into a submarine.

The Royal Navy also had coal-fired ships until the late 1940s. And indeed the Royal Navy developed steam-powered catapults to fly aircraft off Aircraft Carriers replacing the pneumatic system being used at the time. The first ship to use this new design was H.M.S.Perseus an old R.N. Flattop that did sea trials of the coast of the U.S.A. in the late 1950s.

Steam was the main power for many years, in factories; railways and shipping also many of the early cars were steam-powered, Whites being the most famous. One of the first cars to travel at over 100mph in 1920 was steam powered. In 1872 Scottish engineer Charles Randolph of Glasgow built the first engine powered saloon car, with a driver, an engineer-stoker, a boiler, steam engine and coalbunker, the whole vehicle weighting over 4.5 tons. But the main drawback of the steam car was the time taken to raise pressure before it could be used. Steam engines were also used to power the early air-ships, as they were more reliable than the petrol engine at the time, as far back as 1852 Frenchman

H.Giffard flew a steam-driven airship over Paris.

Many different power plants were tried out in aircraft; the Germans had a diesel engine Dornier 215 and Junkers 86 bomber during the war. The Westland Aircraft Company of Yeovil in Somerset successful tested a Bristol built Fredden's Phoenix "1" compression-ignition diesel engine in a Westland Wapiti. A Phoenix "11" supercharged diesel-engine Wapiti "1", with Harald Penrose the Westland test pilot at the controls, on the 14th May 1934 flew to a record height of 28.000 ft (8.535 m).   Subsequently corrected to 27,453 ft. This aircraft had an open cockpit and no heating, Penrose only wore a leather helmet, and kapok padded flying suit and sheepskin gloves. He was breathing neat oxygen from 10,000ft upwards and was bitterly cold the whole time.

A week after the Cabinet meeting Beaverbrook reported back to the P.M. concerning steam powered flight. It was possible to build a steam-powered aeroplane using modern technology. Vospers of Southampton said they could make a steam turbine engine using new materials such a duralumin, light enough to go into an aircraft and with enough power to fly it.

Aviation fuel contains 20.000 BTUs per pound weight and coke, (fuel made from coal,) contains only 15.000 BTUs per pound, (BP. information).

A steam turbine is more efficient than a petrol engine; about 5% better in converting fuel to power and would not suffer from lack of air at altitude. Water would be recovered from the turbines with condensers and returned to the boiler. The total weight of the turbines, water, piping and boiler would be a lot heavier than the normal petrol engines, about 4.000lb more, so that less bombs would be carried using the same weight of fuel. But this was not important when bombing was not the primary duty of the aircraft.

The Vickers Wellington Bomber would be ideal for this with its wide and strong geodetic construction. The boiler was being placed in the middle of the aircraft by the main spar and the coke in bags in the fuselage on five-ply wooden decking. The weight of an empty Wellington was only 16.600lb. The extra weight for the boiler etc. adding 4.000lb. Coke fuel 5.000lb, in 40 bags, 10 in 2 rows 2 high each side of the fuselage, approximately equal in weight to the 750 gallons fuel load of an ordinary Wellington.

The bomb load would be 4 x 250lb bombs and 2 x 250lb, Torpex depth charges. A 250lb bomb exploding within six feet of a submarine would inflict significant damage and the new Torpex-filled depth charge was more practical and successful than the standard Amatol weapon in use at the time and it was also lighter. The total all-up weight of 27.100lb is only 40lb above the normal weight of a Wellington bomber. This extra weight would be used up on raising steam before take off. The only modification was to strengthen the main spar; this is the beam though the wings and the fuselage, as the fuel load were now in the main body of the aircraft and not in the wings. This aircraft could fly 10 to 12 hours at 3.000ft, giving a range of 2.500 to 3.000 miles, on meteorological flights, convoy patrols and submarine hunting etc. over the North Atlantic. Saving valuable aviation petrol and leaving aeroplanes such as the new Avro Lancaster and the American lease-lend Liberators to bomb Germany.

On Sunday 7th December 1941 at 7.55am the Japanese made a surprise attack on Pearl Harbour, sinking nearly the whole of the American Pacific Fleet. 12 ships sunk or beached and 9 damaged including 6 battleships, 323 aircraft damaged or destroyed and 2,395 personnel killed.
The U.S.S. Phoenix was damaged and beached but was later repaired and after the war sold to Argentina and renamed the Belgrano and finally sunk by a British submarine during the Falkland war in 1982.
The same day Japanese bombers destroyed most of the Philippine air force. Three days later on the 10th Dec. Japanese bombers in the South China Sea also sank the British battleship H.M.S. Prince of Wales and the battle cruiser H.M.S. Repulse.

All these events escalated the war and made the project more urgent as petrol was now in very short supply, also the Wellington was becoming redundant as a front line bomber over Europe.
With Churchill's approval, Beaverbrook placed an order in January 1942 for three prototype Steam-powered Wellington bombers.
The parts to be sent to R.A.F. Aldergrove in Northern Ireland to be assembled there by engineers and mechanics from Vickers Aircraft Company and Vospers Marine of Southampton.

The crews were to be sent earlier to gain experience on an old Wellington aircraft, flying long-range navigation flights over the sea, air to sea gunnery and bombing of sea targets.
The crew for each aircraft would be an experienced Pilot, resting from a tour of bombing. A Flight Engineer, who would act as second pilot also to check the steam pressures and water supply etc. a Navigator who would also be the Bomb Aimer, a Wireless Operator/Front Gunner and two Stokers, these were to be seconded from the Royal Navy. They would also act as Rear Gunners, owing to

the shortage of space only one could stoke the boiler at a time. The Admiralty was asked for volunteers from the Stoker Branch of the R.N. to be air gunners in the R.A.F. Out of the many that came forward, thinking this could be a good posting, with more pay and better food, thirteen of the smallest were chosen and sent to Aldergrove in February 1942 to join the rest of the aircrews for training.

The crews were as follows: Crew 1.
Pilot. Flying Officer Desmond "Paddy" Delaney, an Irishman from Donegal where his father kept a pub in Ballyshannon. Aged 30 he was one of the older R.A.F. crewmembers, married with two children, Donna and Mary and lived in the local village with his wife Bridget. He smoked a pipe and was a sombre quiet chap and well liked by all. Just finished a tour of duty on Wellingtons and had been awarded the D.F.C. He had joined the R.A.F. in 1930 and had gone to R.A.F. Halton as an apprentice. Trained as an A.C. electrician then in 1935 transferred to aircrew to be a pilot, then flying Westland Wapitis on the North-west frontier in India, (now on the border of Afghanistan and north Pakistan), helping to keep the peace in the Khyber pass.

Flight Engineer. Sergeant "Robbie" Robinson, age 28, a good looking son of a west country shopkeeper, had gone to one of the minor Public Schools in Somerset, then 9 years as a ground engine mechanic in R.A.F. He then transferred to aircrew and just completed the Flt.Eng. Course at the 4s of T.T. at St Athan in South Wales. "Robbie" could drink every one under the table on a good night and still be bright and breezy the next day, when asked how he felt he always said "great!" On days off he liked to cycle around the green and beautiful countryside of County Antrim, he could play the piano very well and liked to sing but he had a terrible voice.

Navigator/Bomb-Aimer. Flying Officer "Teddy" Bears, D.F.C. ex schoolteacher from a small village school in Dorset, just finished two tours with bomber command. On his last trip the plane had crash-landed on returning to base after being shot up over Holland while dropping leaflets, they all escaped unhurt but for a few scratches.

Wireless Operator/Front Gunner. Sergeant "The Kid" Mann, only 19 years old he as the youngest of all the aircrew. Born in Rochdale in Lancashire, he could play the ukulele very well and had sung on the stage with Gracie Fields but no one dared to call him "Sally". Just finished training and this was his first crew.
The two Navy stokers, were Leading Stoker "Charlie" Hope son of a Yorkshire

coal miner, strong in the arm, thick in the head but a good lad for all that, joined the Navy as a boy seaman, he was always talking about Castleford rugby team.

And L/Stoker "Little Billy" Litton normally known as "Janner", born in the village of Black Dog in the wilds of mid-Devon.

The first time he ever left the village was to join the navy at the age of 15 at the end of the First World War. His family worked for the local Squire where his father was the gardener, his mother "Cook" and as a young boy he ran errands for the Big House, he said that on his 13th birthday the lady of the house, Lady St John-Browne gave him his first very own pair of boots, he was the smallest of all the aircrew.

Crew 2:
Pilot. Sgt. "Joe" Nowocin. Ex-Polish Air Force, he spoke very broken English and most though he was mad, his favourite expression was. "You sink we Polish know noting, but I tell you, I know noting about everything." He was a very good pilot with many hours of flying experience on all types of aircraft.

His father a polish cavalry officer killed in W.W.1 when "Joe" was only five, the rest of his family were killed on the 1st December 1939 in the first Blitzkrieg bombing of the war, when Germany attacked Poland with 1.250.000 men in 60 divisions lead by General Walther Von Brauchitsch.

"Joe" escaped by flying his plane to the south of Sweden where he crashed landed, then made his way to Gothenburg and with aid of the British crew hid aboard a ship to England.

Flight Engineer. Sgt."Johnny" Julier, ex Ford Motors apprentice from Dagenham and the only person to understand "Joe's" English, as his Grandmother was Polish. Johnny was born in Bethnal Green in the Eastend of London in 1920, moved to Dagenham when his father got a job at the new Ford Motors factory in 1935 when Fords moved from Birmingham. "Johnny" was very good at the then new sport in this country of Ju-jitsu.

Nav/Ba. Pilot Officer Alistair "Ally" Smythe, he came from a very wealthy family in the Home Counties, went to Oxford University were he got a "Blue" in fencing. He drove a 1937 Singer nine; some thought he was a bit aloof but he was very clever and could play chess with 6 people at the same time, he could also play chess blindfolded and still win.

W/Op. & Front-Gunner. Sgt. "Nick" Nicholls, who boxed for the R.A.F. before the war, which meant he was not the best looking airman on the station. He liked painting in his spare time and painted the squadron badge but it was never officially accepted.

Air Stokers. L/S."Bill" Rawlins, an old timer who had served on one of the last coal-fired ships in the Royal Navy and on the first purpose-built aircraft carrier the "Ark Royal" but not on the first Ark Royal as some said. And L/S. William Dowell, a fisherman from Weymouth in Dorset, he was know to all as "Portland Bill", joined the R.N. in 1938. His fishing boat had sunk during a storm. A cross-channel ferry from the Channel Islands to Weymouth bringing tomatoes and early potatoes to the English markets saved him and the crew. With no boat he joined the Navy. His home was next to the lifeboat station on Weymouth quay and as a part-time crewman he had often gone out on sea rescues.
Crew 3:
Pilot. F/O. "Ginger" Green, ex fighter pilot, had written off two Hurricanes at Biggin Hill and was sent to Ireland out of the way before he could do any more damage, said he needed glasses as he found it difficult to read the instrument panel in the aircraft.

Flt/Eng. Sgt. "Archie" Parker, a dour Scot from Glasgow. He had helped to build the "Queen Elizabeth" while an apprentice for John Brown on Clyde Bank. He rode an Ariel 500cc motorbike at high speed all around Ulster much to the annoyance of the locals especially when he hit and killed a donkey belonging to an Irish farmer. Luckily Archie was all right but it cost him £5 for the animal.

Nav/Ba. F/O. "Eddie the tash" Edwards, with a large Flying Officer Kite moustache, ex car salesman, a great character who never stopped talking, telling stories or jokes. He had joined up in 1932 during the Depression when trade was very bad. At one time he had played tennis at Wimbledon he was also a very good squash player.
W/Op.F/G. Sgt. "Shiner" Moon, from the Eastend of London where his father was a docker. One of ten children a real cockney sparrow, he had been a barrow boy at one time also a boxer, said he had fought the legendary Freddie Mills in the 1930s in the old Tate & Lyle refinery gym on the north bank of the Thames. "Shiner" could get or scrounge anything but ask no questions as to where it came from. He was a real ladies man and a favourite with all the W.A.A.Fs; occasionally he would have a sparring match with Nick to give a bit of entertainment to the lads.

Stokers. L/S. "Taff" Evans, ex Welsh coal miner, joined the Navy in the 1932 when the Rhondda mine closed in South Wales, he called everyone "boyo". He had played rugby for Pontypridd and Neath at fly-half and had he been bigger would have played for Wales, he had a lovely voice and with "Robbie" on the piano and the "Kid" with his ukulele they put on a great show on Sunday nights in the mess.

And L/S. "Bill" Collard, (my uncle), from Plymouth, served on H.M.S. Exeter at the battle of the River Plate in December 1939 when the German battle ship the Graf Spee was badly damaged by the British cruisers Exeter, Ajax and Achilles. The Graf Spee was scuttled outside Montevideo in Uruguay on Hitler's orders. Many years latter the masts could still be seen sticking out of the water at low tide. The Exeter returned to Devonport very badly damaged but with much celebration and a parade of the crew though the streets of the City.
Uncle Bill's father, great uncle Dick had sailed before the mast on the old time sailing ships at the turn of the century, now retired he grew tobacco in his back garden at Piccadilly in one of the cottages opposite the Blackbird pub just outside Wellington in Somerset. Piccadilly is a name given to a row of dwellings on the edge of a town, even in London at the time.

The Spare stoker was Able Seaman Pedro "The Daggo" Ormrod, his father was a merchant seaman from Liverpool and his mother Portuguese, they meet when Pedro's father went on a ship to bring port from Oporto to Bristol in 1919. Pedro spoke perfect Portuguese but "Scouse" English. A bit of a footballer and liked to box until he was well and truly beaten by Nick and Shiner.

A spare crew was also sent, they were as follows.
Pilot. Flying Officer "Jimmy" Wilson, M.M. T.D. He had joined the Territorial Army in 1937, learnt to fly at his own expense and joined the R.A.F. in early 1939. Went to France with the British Expeditionary force flying in a Taylorcraft, the predecessor of the Auster built by the Slingsby Aircraft Company in Rearsby Leicester. He was shot down while spotting for the Royal Artillery over Belgium. He escaped to Dunkirk and was evacuated back to England on a small Thames riverboat. Given a desk job which he hated he transferred to Bomber Command with the chance he might continue flying.

Flight Engineer. Sgt. "Curly" Swaffield, his father had a garage in Bristol and they still had the Model "T" Ford his father learnt to drive on in 1915. "Curly" was a very good mechanic always helping others with their cars and motorbikes, he drove a big Morris 12 and was a excellent driver.
But for the war he had hoped to become a top class-racing driver as he had

driven at Brooklands in the 1930s. He was also mechanic to Sir Henry Segrave the leading racing driver of that era, who set the world land speed record of 231mph in 1929 and was killed on Lake Windermere in 1930 while setting the new world water speed record of 98.76mph. He also held many air-speed records.

Nav/Ba. Pilot Office "Chalky" White. Just joined the Air Force from one of the new Universities and knew it all. Round as he was tall which was not very much, some times called "Rolly" from the way he walked.
The best laugh was had when he fell off of his bike, he didn't know that some one had undone the wheel nuts.
W.Op. Sgt. "Nobby" Bignall, sometimes known as "Sparky". A small chap from Newport Pagnell, his father worked for the London Midland & Scottish Railway engine works in Wolverton. "Nobby's" hobby was bell ringing and on Sundays went to the local church where he helped to waken the whole neighbourhood with the clanging of the bells. The Wops were always talking to each other in Morse code much to the annoyance of the others that couldn't understand it.

The two stokers were. L/S. "Jock" McNeil. A coal miner from Motherwell in Scotland, he played football for Glasgow Rangers before he joined up. His broad Glaswegian accent was worse than "Joe's" Polish English, and Able Seaman "Digger" Yates. He had been to Australia once as a merchant seaman and never stopped talking about it and something called St. Elmo's fire. He transferred to the Royal Navy at the outbreak of the war.

The new bombers were being assembled in the end hangar guarded night and day by armed Military Police (snow drops), no one was allowed near, the workers lived in separate quarters and were sworn to silence. Much speculation was made, but the general opinion (the latest gen) was that they were being fitted with new anti-submarine radar. At the end of Marsh the crews were paraded and Marched by Ft.Sgt. "Daisy" May to the hangar and taken inside. Three brand new shiny Wellington Bombers stood in the hangar. The tall tube on the top of the fuselage and the bulbous lump below confirmed their opinion that it was the new radar, but they were surprised at seeing the new sleek engines. They were then assembled in the Operations Room. On the wall was a large diagram of the new aircraft. The Commanding Officer, Group Captain Sir Charles de Flanders D.F.C. & bar. M.C. O.B.E. Ex Royal Flying Corps pilot from the First World War when he had lost an eye then explained the new and unique design of this aircraft. It was fuelled by COKE and driven by STEAM!

The room was in uproar. The C.O. removed his monocle and called for silence, he then went into the finer details of the new aircraft.

The crews were stunned. He then asked if there were any question, all the sailors shouted that they wanted to go back to sea. The navy lads had been unhappy from the start, because they were not getting their rum ration which would have been 1/8 of a pint of rum mixed with 1/4 pint of water per day, known as "grog". This was issued to all sailors below the rank of Petty Officer in the Royal Navy. Non-commission officers received 1/8 of a pint of rum without water known as "neaters". This was not allowed on a R.A.F. Station. But if a soldier or airman was on board ship or even a R.N. shore base they were allowed to partake and the other moan was they were still only getting their Navy pay plus 3d (1.5p) in lieu of the rum tot. But they were all told that you can volunteer for a new posting but you cannot unvolunteer and must stick with it.

The next day all the crews were assembled to test their new aircraft. Air Stoker A/S Ormrod was missing. They later received a postcard from Rio de Janeiro saying he had gone to Liverpool, got a ship to South America and had joined the Brazilian Navy.

At 9.30am all the aircraft were ground tested and with a light fuel load at 10.30am on the 1st April 1942   Airsteam 1 with "Paddy" Delaney at the controls took off and flew three circuits of the Aerodrome and landed with lots of cheering and much relief all around.

The other aircraft followed soon after and the rest of the day was taken up with air testing, trials and circuit & bumps. There were a few complaints from some local housewives about spots of soot on their washing but were told it was oil from the new engines and they were issued with bars of N.A.A.F.I. soap as a peace offering.

Many flights were made in the coming weeks. One of the hardest jobs was for the W.Op to wind the funnel down by hand for take off to reduce the drag and back draft to the boiler, this took 200 turns of a wheel with a handle on. The top of the fuselage behind the funnel had a metal plate to stop the fabric from catching fire from the sparks. The ashes from the firebox came out of a vent under the aircraft and were discharged downwards into the slipstream. Some times on a long flight the stokers cooked bacon on their shovels and provided bacon butties for the crew. The boiler had a hot water container so that they could also make tea.

Occasionally the pilots tried to help the stokers by putting the aircraft into a dive so that the bags of coke could be moved forward easier. The new Wellingtons handled extremely well and the only modification was to add a steam reservoir to give extra power for take off and over shooting.

The crews had a great time in Northern Ireland. Saturday dances at the station and at the local pub where much Guinness was drunk on many occasions. One night "Paddy" lost his false teeth down the toilet and they were never seen again, unfortunately it took several weeks to get a new set so he couldn't smoke his pipe. "Robbie" chatted up the bar maid at the local pub, the daughter of the Landlord "Mick" Magee, a blue eyed dark haired beauty named Philomena but being a Catholic she had to go to confession every Sunday and tell all to the priest. She was very well endowed and the crews changed the name of their life jackets from Mae West to Phil West.

"Johnny" went out with a W.A.A.F called Chrissie from the medical section; they were lucky for on a cold night they could sit in the ambulance where it was nice a warm. "Taffy" married a Y.M.C.A tea girl named Chloe and moved into married quarters, and "Ally" married "Dusty" Brown a W.A.A.F. parachute packer, a very pretty girl who was admired by all but he had a car and money, they moved into the nearby hotel.

At the end of May the three planes went on active service, joining No 15 Group Coastal Command flying over the North Atlantic on Met. Flights, Convoy Patrols and Sub. Hunting. Two U-boats were attacked and one believed to have been sunk.

The Battle of the Atlantic was becoming graver. Admiral Doenitz said, "The gloves were off" when The United States entered the war. In three weeks in early 1942, 40 US ships were sunk and in the first six months 585 allied ships, over 3.000.000 tons went to the bottom of the Atlantic. In May 109 ships sunk off the East Coast of America including 30 oil tankers. 91 U-boats were operating in the first two months of 1942, 111 by Marsh and 140 at the end of June.

The project seemed on the whole a great success and on the 21st June 1942 18 more Wellington steam-powered aircraft were ordered, and two new squadrons were to be formed one based at Aldergrove and the other at Kinloss in Scotland, to join 15 Group Coastal Command.

Then on the 28th July came the first crash. A.S.1 was on take off and climbing away when the steam pressure valve jammed. The pilot sent out a "Mayday" call and the flight engineer hit the valve several times with a big spanner, but minutes later at 500ft the aircraft blew up, killing all the crew except one of the stokers who was sat in the rear turret and managed to bale out. He only suffered a broken ankle but was so shocked that his hair went white and he spent the rest of his life in a mental home and the only sound he ever made again was to sing, "The runaway train came over the hill and she blew".

On the 31st August 1942, A.S.2 was on a Met. Flight out over the Atlantic when a steam pipe started to leak, the flight engineer badly burning his hands tried wrapping insulation tape around the pipe and also using a jubilee clip to try and stop the steam leaking out. The boiler continued to lose pressure and water.

The crew put all the liquid they could find into the tank. One of the stokers tied a bucket to a rope to try to get some seawater but was dragged out of the aircraft and drowned. One mile from the coast the engines ran out of steam and they ditched the aircraft into the sea.

Some Irish fishermen who were close by rescued the rest of the crew and they were interned in Southern Ireland. They escaped one Saturday night when all the Guards were drunk and they made it back over the border to the North and rejoined the group.

On the 21st September, A.S.3 coming back from a long anti-submarine patrol over the North Atlantic met very strong head winds and ran low on fuel. The crew put anything that would burn into the boiler, even their flying boots and the wooden decking, they made it back to the airfield but unfortunately on approaching the runway they were struck by a strong cross wind. The pilot tried to over-shoot but ran out of power and landed in Lough Neagh the large lake near Aldergrove.

The crew was O.K. but for my Uncle Bill who broke his knee. They all got into the dinghy and made it to the shore and back to camp, wet and bedraggled carrying my uncle between them. He had a stiff leg for the rest of his life.

By the end of September 1942 the Battle of the Atlantic was being won. Fewer ships were sunk, more oil was arriving, The R.A.F. were bombing the submarine pens on the continent and the Royal Navy destroyers, corvettes and Coastal Command were sinking many U-boats.

The U.S.A. was supplying Great Briton with Liberator bombers and Catalina flying boats. Coastal Command with the new American aircraft using bases in Newfoundland, Iceland and Ireland had many successes and sank a great many of the enemy submarines. Especially successful was the new Leigh Light Wellington. This had a large searchlight powered by a Ford V8 engine pointing down at the sea and caught many submarines at night on the surface when they were recharging their batteries.

The Catalina could fly 3.000 miles and stay in the air for 27 hours; they could fill up with fuel in the Caribbean and patrol the whole of the Atlantic in one flight. A Lease-Lend R.A.F. Catalina flying boat with a Canadian crew, hunting the Bismarck in May 1941 had been the first to spot the German ship. They had remained on patrol for 27 hours and must have flown over 3,000 miles in the course of that tour of duty.

The night of 23rd October 1942 the 8th Army under General Montgomery started the Battle of El Alamein where the German army lead by Field Marshal Rommel was finally stopped. The battle for Egypt had been won the Suez Canal and the Middle East oil fields were saved. This was the turning point of the war. Churchill said at the Lord Mayor's Banquet at the Mansion House in London on the 10th November 1942.
"This is not the end, it is not even the beginning of the end, but it is perhaps, the end of the beginning".

On the 15th November the Steam Wellington project was cancelled, the ordered aircraft were fitted with petrol engines and were sent to India to help with Burma campaign. The remaining crews were sent back to their units and for fear of being laughed at never mentioned the project to anyone.

My uncle went to Devonport and was given light duties in the dockyard and many will remember him riding his bike with one leg and for better support had a car steering wheel instead of handlebars. Very few of the other crewmembers survived the war.
"Jimmy" Wilson went on to fly Lysanders, especially flying to France on moonlit nights taking and bringing back our agents also taking supplies to the underground army the Maquis. He crashed-landed in northern France just after D.Day and was hidden by a French farmer until he was rescued by the British troops, he wasn't happy on being rescued as he was getting on very well with the farmer's daughter. He became one of the first British officers to enter Paris on the 26th August 1944 just behind General de Gaulle as he Marched down the Champs Elysees at the head of the Free French army.

After the war my uncle emigrated to Australia on the S.S. Canberra with the £10 assisted passage scheme, he died in 1990 aged over 80 in Melbourne. His son Clifford sent me his diaries of the war in 1993 to try and confirm the events. But the only evidence is perhaps a Wellington bomber at the bottom of Lough Neagh in Northern Ireland with a coke boiler in the middle of the fuselage and a few half burnt flying boots, one day perhaps a diving team may find it.

The Government records have never been released possibly for fear of disbelief or ridicule. The project was top secret during the war as the Germans and Japanese were also short of petrol and may have used the idea.

It is thought that the Germans tried using powdered coal under very high steam pressure and oxygen in their experimental jet fighters or rocket aircraft at the end of the war but all records was destroyed in the allied bombing. The R.A.F. Experimental Establishment at Farnborough also tried using powdered coal in jet engines for ground generators but they became clogged up with tar. However, the story that the fire bomb raid on Hamburg was caused by steam powered Wellingtons raking out their cinders over the city is not true, nor did the wings flap up & down powered steam pistons as some thought.

This is a strange and unusual story of World War Two taken from my uncle's diaries. The facts and figures have been checked and as far as I can ascertain the story is true.

P.S. Some of the names have been changed to save their families from any distress. The details of the Battle of the Atlantic were taken from R.A.F.A. AIR MAIL MAG. Spring 1993.

This story is dedicated to. That happy band, that chosen few.

The Royal Naval Air Stokers of, 42.

Who with the Royal Air Force flew.

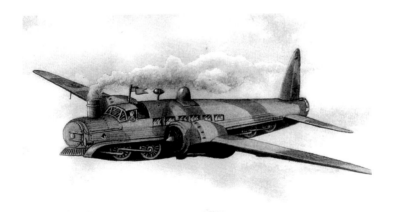

An artist's impression of a steam powered Wellington Bomber 1942

Memories of the Author during the Second World War 1939-1945 in Yeovil

I was born in 1932. July the 28th. Above the corner shop my parents kept at 2 Beer Street in Yeovil. I was aged seven and two months when War was declared on Sunday the 3rd September 1939. I remember sitting around the table at home listening with my Mum and Dad to The Prime Minister Mr. Chamberlain speaking on the wireless set. His final words '—This Country is now at war with Germany.' Sent a chill through the room and we all went very quiet.

My memory before that was of a German airship going over Yeovil at a great height, we all stood in the street, looking up at this long silver shape as it travelled East to West. I understand later that it was taking photographs of southern England. (More of this later.) As a Cub Scout I helped fill sand bags as men dug trenches where the Octagon Theatre is now and I acted as a casualty for an air raid exercise with a label tied to me saying I had been gassed!!
The first Christmas of the War I was given a Morse code machine, my only present, so that I could learn how to send messages.

We all went to Hendford Manor to collect our gas masks; we had special lessons at school to see how quickly we could put them on. The brown cardboard box they came in with string to go around the neck was useful; with two sticks it made a very good drum as we Marched up and down the street beating our drums and singing 'The British Grenadiers', I wore a tin hat I bought from Woolworth's for six pence (2.5p). My brother, Cliff, thought he would test it and hit me on the head with a big stick making a dent in the helmet and knocking me out, mother then hit him with the stick across his behind.

Many soldiers were stationed in Yeovil, empty houses were requisitioned and lots of troops camped on the Fair Field in Salt house Lane and where the Post Office is in Huish. It was quite a sight to see brengun carriers going round the streets churning up the tarmac. A Scottish piper, a very strange noise to us, sounded early morning reveille.

They then left for France at the end of 1939 with the British Expedionary Force. Later I remember many ladies going to Yeovil Junction Railway Station to serve tea and cakes to the soldiers returning from Dunkirk.

The first bomb to fall in the area, as I recall, was in a field between the Half Way

Inn and Ilchester, all the boys cycled out to see the hole in the ground and tried to find some bits of shrapnel, the next one was in Derryman's field where Morrison's Superstore now stands, another expedition to find souvenirs.

It was very exciting to see Westland Lysanders flying overhead and looking at them parked on the County Cricket Ground where Westland Engineers are at the end of West Hendford. My brother was an apprentice at Westland's, he made control columns for Lysanders in a small workshop in the under ground car park below the cattle market next to the Odeon cinema in Court Ash.

Westland Aircraft Works was camouflaged as a housing estate before the war, windows, doors and chimney pots painted on the buildings. I think the photos taken by the airship before the war confused the Germans and they got it the wrong way round, for when the bombing really started they bombed north instead south of the airfield on 8th Oct. 1940 hitting Preston Grove, Westbourne Close, Westbourne Grove, killing Mrs. Harrison whose husband had a grocery shop on the corner. They also hit Grove Avenue, and St Andrews Road where you can still see the marks on the walls of the houses. I was taking our dog for a walk along West Hendford towards Westlands; it was just a stone track and garden allotments then. When the bombs started falling, I ran for home on the corner of Beer Street, men were lying on the pavement against the wall and shouting, 'get down you silly b----,' but I kept running, I was going home to mum.

We had our windows blown out several times, the blackout curtains thrown across the room and the ceilings brought down; these were repaired with Essex Boarding, sheets of fibreboard Dad bought from Bradford's building merchants. When the air-raid siren sounded, mum, dad and myself sheltered under the stairs as it was thought the safest place. My brother wouldn't get out of bed, he said, ' I'd sooner go down with the rubble than be buried under it.'

My father was in the Railway Hotel in Hendford when the skittle alley at the back was hit and he was very upset as bottles of whisky fell off the shelves and broke as he was lying on the floor against the Bar.

I well remember when Burtons fifty shillings Tailors in Middle Street was hit on the 7th Oct 1940 and for ages the whole front of the building was open to the elements with the light bulb still dangling from the ceiling. I was asleep in bed when Boots the chemist, (now Burger King,) was bombed in the middle of the night on Good Friday 11th April 1941, I was thrown out of bed by the massive explosion and onto the floor, wondering what had happened. I think it was a delayed action bomb

I was sent to Bridport to stay with friends of the family called Chant who had a bakery there to escape the bombing only to have that town bombed while I was there. I nearly went to Canada with the children's evacuation scheme but would not go. Just as well as because one of the ships taking the children across the Atlantic was sunk by a U-Boat and hundreds was drowned.

Because of the danger of the school being hit and many children being killed at the same time we had our lessons in the teacher's houses, they lived locally in those days; our class went to Mrs. Berryman's house in 93 West Hendford. Others went to Mrs. Field's; her husband had a bakery in Wellington Street and Mrs. Trask a member of the local mineral water company.

Evacuees came to Yeovil from London and quite a few went at our school, Huish where Tesco's petrol station now stands. These 'Cockneys' were very strange to us, pale, thin but very street-wise, a bit of a cultural shock to us. They definitely knew more about the birds and the bees than us country kids, but they didn't know where milk came from. One of the strange events of those days when we had PT. (Physical Training), the boys had to take off their shirts and the girls had to remove their dresses.
Well one of the London girls, Julie who was quite a big girl, wouldn't take off her thin cotton dress, teacher said 'Julie take off your dress at once.'
'I don't want to Miss,' she replies, almost in tears.
'I said take it off, now do it, at once.' Demanded the teacher.
With that, Julie removed the garment, only to reveal that she had no underwear. The poor girl was very embarrassed, the lady went as red as a beetroot and said, 'Put that dress back on at once, you naughty girl. The rest of you outside now.' Julie put her dress back on. But us boys just looked agog, with our mouths wide open. In those more innocent days it was the first time many of us had ever seen a naked girl. I thought girls were just boys with long hair, so began my first lesson in sex education.

The small grocery shop opposite us in West Hendford was owned by Mr. Freke but he was a Major in the Territorial Army and he went off to war leaving it empty so the Authorities put three mothers with their children in there, they had been evacuated from the Channel Islands.
When the air-raid siren went when we were at school we had to go to the shelter at the bottom of the play ground and sit in rows on wooden benches in the dark but it wasn't too bad because I made sure I sat next to Janet who I really liked and I could hold her hand if I thought she was frightened.
During the time of the German invasion scare after Dunkirk, barbed wire and

pillboxes surrounded Yeovil, one was at the top of Hendford Hill it was disguised as a gazebo (demolished in 2006) and another on Summer House hill. The road by our shop had two big concrete pillars on the pavement and metal covers across the road to put bent railway lines in to stop enemy tanks.

Soldiers dug a machine gun post at the bottom of Seaton Road and a young officer came into our shop and wanted to knock a hole in our upstairs front room for a machine gun as it faced the open fields opposite. My mum, Ada, soon told him what to do.

The whole town was a Redoubt or defensive system for a last stand between Lyme Regis and Bristol and East of the Country. Maiden Newton was also a Redoubt town.
I carved the Union Jack image in the brickwork of the shop doorway with a nail just in case the Germans occupied us.

In the hit and run raid on the 5th August 1942 two German Focke-Wulf 190 fighter-bombers went past my bedroom window at rooftop height as I was going to bed, I saw the black cross and the swastika on the side of the planes not more than fifty feet from the window. Mum, who was drawing the curtains shouted 'get under the bed'.

They then dropped bombs on Grass Royal, Gordon Road and Dampier Street damaging several hundred houses. In all the raids on Yeovil 49 people were killed 122 injured not including some soldiers killed at Houndstone Camp. But Westland Aircraft Works only once received some slight damage. During the War 46 were killed in Weymouth by the bombing. 18 people were killed in Sherborne on the 30th September 1940, when a German bomber force mistook it for Yeovil because of very heavy cloud cover. As far as I can recall no one was killed in Bridport or Dorchester, but 219 were killed in Bournemouth due to bombing during W.W.2.

Many thousand of American Soldiers, (I think over 10,000) were stationed in and around Yeovil prior to D.Day, at Barwick Park, Hounstone camp, The Fair Ground in Salt House Lane, Martock, Bradford Abbas, Mudford also many houses in Yeovil were requisitioned They were very generous to the local children giving us food, sweets and chewing gum.

The call was. 'Got any gum chum.) Also 'K' rations (boxes of mixed food etc for emergencies.) And nylons for girls, how and why these men came to have stockings in their kit bags was a mystery to us young boys.

They were young and very friendly; I remember some coming to our house for Sunday tea. One sergeant came from Boston Massachusetts; I think he had a Polish name. He gave me some postage stamps from his hometown.

It was quite exiting when they collected the pay roll for their troops from Lloyds Bank in the Borough once a month. An armoured car pulled up outside the bank, which was then surrounded by American military policemen with colt 45s on their belts and Tommy guns at the ready, just like the movies, very heady stuff. One night the Yanks tried to drive a jeep down lovers lane and it got stuck half way and they had to reverse all the way back.

My father; Harold Robins had a paper shop on the corner of Beer Street. I was not quite twelve years old and every afternoon after school I cycled up Hendford Hill to Barwick Park selling the Evening Standard to the American soldiers, I had a special pass signed by the Camp Commander. There were about five thousand camped there, all very young and friendly. Then one day in early June I went to the camp after school and they had all left, the whole place was completely empty. No one had told me it was D.Day! But I still managed to sell the papers to all and sundry, shouting. 'Invasion in Europe imminent!' Before I got back to the shop. Although it wasn't actually in the papers I had to sell them, otherwise dad would be cross.

I now understand they all went to Weymouth on Sunday night and many embarked for 'Omaha' beach on coast of Normandy in France, where they sustained the highest losses. The total on June 6th was 5,400 casualties of which 'Omaha' beach had 2,400 including 1,000 killed on the first day, some of the same young men I had sold papers and talked to only a few days before, so very sad.

On the Wednesday afternoon of the invasion we were playing cricket on our school playing field where the Golden Stones swimming pool is now situated and the whole time bombers, Dakota transport planes and aircraft towing gilders were passing overhead towards France, it was an amazing sight with broad white stripes like pigeons painted on the wings to show they were allied aircraft.

The end of the war in Europe was a bit of an anti climax; black out restrictions had been lifted on the 18th September 1944. The war in the Far East against Japan still went on, shortages and rationing became worse, bread and potatoes were added, even chickens were a luxury. Rationing did not finally end till the 1950s. Shortages still went on, power cuts, water turned off at night, I didn't taste tinned fruit until I went to Egypt in 1952 with the R.A.F. During my National Service. Hard times… but at least we were alive.

One of the lasting memories of that time was the British prisoners of war coming home, especially from the Far East, thin, pale, some yellow skinned. One said I never ever wanted rice again. Although glad to be home they remained depressed for a long time. Perhaps thinking of their lost youth and the friends they had left behind buried in some foreign field.

Tony with his dog Whisky, Aldon House Road 1944